Jagger's Revolution

KEVIN HUNTER

WARRIOR
OF LIGHT
PRESS

Los Angeles, California

Jagger's Revolution is semi-autobiographical, but a work of fiction. Some names, events and places have been exaggerated in certain scenarios. Being able to tell what is true and what isn't is impossible as it is seamlessly woven together. This book is not for the easily offended as the content is sexually graphic and explicit in places.

Warrior of Light Press
Dude Literature. www.kevin-hunter.com

Romance. Drama. Erotica. Gay. Young Adult.

PRODUCTION CREDITS:
Copy Editor: James Szopo

Interior dark photograph of shirtless guy:
Kahil Nettleton © Copyright 2011
www.spiderflystudios.com
and
Photography by Nadejda Churco ©Copyright 2011
Shivary.deviantart.com

Painting photo in the last pages of the book by, Joshua Shotwell
© Copyright 2006

ISBN-13: 978-0692305034
ISBN-10: 0692305033

Author's Note

Jagger is my alter ego and one of the many selves that live within me. *Jagger's Revolution* is a semi-autobiographical book or what one could call 'faction'. Some of the scenarios described in the essays in this book are true accounts of my dating, sex and relationship life in the past, while others are exaggerated with thrown in drama. This book was written in 2004-2005. It has been available to the public since the end of 2006. However, in 2014 there were a few lines that were removed the book. This is due to the distributor finding the words to be 'crossing the line'. What's been removed is minor and doesn't take away from the overall point of this story. There are a great deal of books out there that far exceed the content that exists in this book. This book is tepid in comparison to what's out there. Although *Jagger's Revolution* might be considered offensive to some, I've only seen this book as a love story and nothing more. I'm a romantic at heart and a love addict after all. Sometimes you have to undergo a good deal of poor date prospects before you connect with the lifelong relationship mate. In a romantic comedy or romantic drama movie, the audience is aware that the two people will end up together, but what is exciting is the buildup along the journey before that happens. That's what *Jagger's Revolution* is about. It's enjoying the rough ride before the pay off connection happens between Jagger and Garth. This occurs in the final chapters sixteen through nineteen *(pgs. 161-219)*. I reveal this now for those readers unable to suffer through the buildup wondering if Jagger will ever obtain his crush. Enduring the journey is necessary to grasp the final impact. Jagger is one guy's quest to find a meaningful love connection with one person that lasts a lifetime. I realize this is no longer the popular view considering that there are now more single people in the United States alone than those who are in a relationship. This points to an even greater issue that's taking place with humanity as a whole.

~ Kevin Hunter

Chapters

Jagger's
Revolution

CHAPTER 1

The Crush

It's an unusual heat wave in March in the city of Hermosa Beach, California. This is home to the surfer's walk of fame and where the too sexy it should be illegal cascade along the beach playing volleyball or surfing the cosmic Pacific Ocean waves. A young, rebellious man breathes down its neck pulling out its sexual diversity without so much as a word. Jagger careens around the corner at lightning speed leaving a trail blazed behind him. His black pick-up truck dominates a street lined with cactus for a block and a half where the foot of the beach starts. He is consumed with all sorts of mental breakage while yammering away on the phone. Lethal and territorial with his crowd and environment, there is an easy vibe about him mixed with a dangerous edge.

He finds a spot between a parked corolla and a small trashcan on wheels that stands in his way. He battles with reversing his truck into a small open space available to parallel park. Feeling destructive and antsy like he can do anything he wants, he attempts to back the truck up into the spot around the trash can. God forbid he climbs out to move the trash receptor. That's not his style. If something is in his way, then he hits it or runs over it.

There is a rough beauty about him that is aloof and attractive. He is a loner and a tough guy with a warrior's edge. There are cuts and scars on him from running and jumping off high objects to temper his occasional unruly aggression. He's crashed down onto the street and pavement more than once. Thirty-two years old with looks in the mid-20's, his endless active lifestyle has done him good. He gets into the occasional fist-fight, but is merely trying to survive standing up for a fair Prince or Princess in a jam. He doesn't know why he gives a shit for humankind, as man hasn't been kind to him or each other. As a sex columnist and on an intellectual level he hates stereotypes and doesn't agree with them. Pigeonholes and labels are both offensive and repetitive in his mind.

He reverses the truck and his back tire hikes up onto the curb. Accelerating forward abruptly and slamming on the brakes causes a loud echoing screech. He slams his truck into the trashcan causing it to spin around while an onlooker watches concerned in the distance. Paying no mind, he backs up banging the tire against the curb.

"What the fuck." He says under his breath. He hits the steering wheel with his palms in a brash manner.

Slamming on the gas he runs into the trash can once more.

"Hold on." He shouts into his earpiece then, "Let me call you back!"

The driver door swings open and a huge beach breeze rushes past the truck. Jagger's hiking boot hits the street pavement hard. With combative movements he climbs out of the car into plain view. He is about medium height, not ultra short or tall, but to some it's known as the fun height. He's got a classically young looking face and body, a short dark military hair cut and huge killer brown eyes. Testosterone radiates off of his body which is strong and confident. Although a regular guy he permeates heavy doses of mystery and superiority. He sports khaki shorts and a camouflage tank top with the words "ARMY" on the front and "FUCK" on the back.

His shorts hang casually over his ass, which is full and round. His ass makes some heterosexual guys drool and secretly fantasize what it would be like if they experimented once. They would never go through with it with another guy, but they can't control their imagination. Instead they direct their focus for a second at the smoky dude and wonder. They attempt to wipe away the fantasy so as not to grow a hard on and have to explain it to their girlfriends, friends or themselves. Only when he's a largely evolved hetero guy who is sure of himself will it rarely bother him.

Jagger marches like a sergeant with frenetic energy grabbing onto the handle of the trash can. He drags it away onto the sidewalk. It makes a deathly echo into the air of the neighborhood. He is here and making himself known. A tone about him is intimidating. Some beach folks walk by uncomfortable rushing past him quickly.

He hikes back to the truck and stares face forward horrified. Butterflies swarm around in his stomach and his heart pounds faster in a rare vulnerability. He wants to be shot dead right there on the street like a mountain lion that shouldn't be roaming around the city. Everything stops around him and nothing else matters. Mesmerized by the new guy in his town he's had a crush on since he first saw him. Getting Jagger to feel any crushing feelings on anyone is impossible, but he feels an uncontrollable connection to this one. It isn't difficult to know why when you cross paths with the sweetest guy on the planet.

Garth stands half a block away in his own tracks eyeing Jagger. Garth's mouth moves half open in fear and wonderment. His messy dirty blonde hair blows a little in the wind. His deep green eyes pierce into Jagger's heart. Every shade of Jagger's face becomes etched into Garth's mind. He has red lifeguard shorts on and shirt while holding a surfboard under his arm. He's a different wild animal than Jagger, but untamed and unruly nonetheless.

Both dudes stand in stillness unable to move in the city jungle wondering if the other is a friend or threat they would need to fight to the death. There's no greater feeling than having a hot crush on someone, but there's no worse feeling when the one you're crushing on has no idea. Neither are aware that they're both thinking the same thing about the other.

Jagger's breath leaves him and the guy's cavernous eyes pound all over his body. It's as if an unknown entity is reaching down his throat with strong fingers and drawing the air out of his shaking soul. Jagger has a soft spot for this guy, amidst his own menacing aura that people first see.

They both look away and at each other and then away. It's the typical shy school boy stance when crossing paths with a crush.

Garth continues on his walk down the slight slope knowing he will pass Jagger from across the street.

Jagger wants to die. *'Fuck me. I have to complicate things by falling for someone.'*

Garth senses Jagger's eyes burning deep into him as he gets close enough to plant the grenade. He works up the courage to be neighborly. "Hey." His voice is gritty and rough, but he lights up like an angel. He could talk a man into turning himself into the law and starting his life over in a better way. Garth's voice sounds like he is hanging onto what's left of his teenage puberty, but he's twenty-four years old and this is his voice. Pushing six feet, he towers Jagger by just enough to overpower him if he wanted to. Garth has a noticeable Aussie accent and is the most stunning creature Jagger has ever seen. Jagger no longer has to worry about trying to write about love he has when he doesn't have any. He's found his muse and damn inspiration.

Jagger remains cool, low and raspy when he responds, "Hello." His voice soothes Garth's world and cradles it. Garth trembles slightly with a nod as he passes him and continues on down to the crowded beach. The white sands and blue sea up ahead is the spot that Garth would make love to Jagger every day all day and night if he could. Having a crush on someone hurts because it often feels like it's not shared. This is why it's a crush, because it crushes you. You feel vulnerable and stupid as if you are alone in the equation. Turning the feelings off is near impossible as you have no idea why you feel this way so intensely. You wish you could turn it off so that you can relax and be cool. Your crush might notice you more when they see your strong poise, instead of the disappointment, all thumbs aura and pain that rises whenever that person is in your vicinity.

Jagger climbs back into his truck to absorb Garth's energy. He sits for a moment exhaling and glancing up without lifting his head. Garth is in the distance heading down to the beach and Jagger feels guilty for looking. He places both hands on the steering wheel and leans his head over exhaling again. "Fuck."

Garth is one of the hottest lifeguards on the beach. Jagger uses every free second available to be consumed with thoughts of him. He wonders about this guy to help him sleep throughout the night with sweet images of the two of them together. Daydreaming of what it would be like to have him as part of his life. This could be the Father of his kids! The way Garth moves and the discipline he conveys inside and out that very few guys have in Jagger's eyes lures him in even more.

Sometimes Garth goes for a run and his well-built body, his tight and toned legs, chest and arms seep through his shorts and his shirt if he has one on. Jagger's eyes make out every inch and shape of it all in hot eroticism. His arms. His ass. He wonders what his cock would look like and what he would look like naked. He wants to run his fingers through the little dark blonde hairs on his legs and let all of them stand up and take notice of him.

Jagger goes running too and every now and then the guys near pass each other while on their walk or jog, but those moments are far and few between. It is all set up on divine timing when they'll bump into one another next. They already have a common ground. They both like to take care of themselves. Jagger doesn't have to worry about some dude who enjoys getting sloshed all night at a club or bar on a regular basis destroying his health, looks, whole aura and being. He can't handle the instability and neurosis associated with someone who cannot make it a week without having a drink.

Garth watches Jagger with his mouth open ready to take his lips in. He stands there in heat holding a fork and knife ready to go to town. Sometimes Garth catches Jagger when he is outside or on his balcony on the street that commands the neighborhood as if he secretly owns it, but tells no one. Garth gazes at him gaping in heavy teen love angst as if they are both fifteen, horny and in love. He searches for the push to make his voice heard in his direction. If he weren't so damn good looking, he would be blended into the wall, an observer, a solid, quiet one with an active spirit.

Jagger knows Garth is the fucking ultimate babe, but tries desperately to get back to planet earth and snap out of it. He's tired of hallucinating as if he has a shot with him. There is a nasty twinge in his side that convinces him that Garth doesn't know he exists. He's left with feeling like the daily idiot he's perfected so well whenever around him. He wants to be hosed down with cold water and maybe it'll go away. Alleviate it off his body the way a car's radiator steams out of the sides of the hood when it's used every ounce of liquid it has. Yet, he loves the way Garth watches him. It seems like he's in love with him. He wants to believe that the guy is attracted to him. Garth stares at him as if he's never seen anyone like him before. He sees him and sees who his soul truly is. Jagger sometimes catches Garth watching him. It drives him nuts and he coyly looks anywhere else, but at him. He masturbates to thoughts of him with the Summer night breeze rushing into the living room of his home enveloping his body that drips with beads of sweat. Garth's hands grabbing hold of Jagger's body and kissing down it methodically.

Jagger jolts back to reality and hops out of his truck bummed out that it isn't real.

Cars and trucks pull onto the street to park. They are crammed with surfboards sticking out of their trunks or strapped onto the top of the cars. Hot beach dudes and the occasional hot beach chick pull their surfboards out of their vehicles. One by one they catch a glimpse of Jagger and smile. They wave captivated knowing this is his home too. They all assume a friendship on that tidbit alone. Jagger slams the door to his truck closed and smiles at one of his local surf buds he recognizes in the bunch. Trezner smiles back and heads over to Jagger.

Jagger hi-fives Trezner with a fist bump, "Hey man, you know they don't let faggots surf here."

Trezner wraps his arm tight around Jagger, "What's up bitch? I'm taking a break from the Malibu swells. How have they been here this week?"

"In Hermosa baby, there are never any disappointments. The waves have been blowin' up the last couple days." Jagger's eyes drift out to sea on the sidewalk in the distance where Garth was not long before. The sidewalk path sparkles with light where his earth angel had passed. Trezner smirks smitten by Jagger who is oblivious by the attention.

Jagger trips, stumbles and falls flat on his face with his dating tribulations. He gets paid to do it. He writes essay pieces of his trek on the rocky road to finding love for a hip and cool pop cultural magazine. It's geared mostly towards 20's and 30's single folks who are in the dating game hoping to pounce on a mate like an animal, but all ages are welcome. He has his own relationship column or the less conservative terminology: Sex Column.

He's jumped off a ten story building and survived with what he drags himself through on a weekly basis. It's worth it to gain experience and knowledge about human behavior in his line of work. You learn things not through classes, but through life's practice.

The thing is the other people he meets on his dating excursions are troubled in many ways. Some have their never ending quest for sex and others are perpetually ruined over their past dating experiences. They take those bad incidents with them on every potential conquest meeting. This gets them nowhere, but results in additional wounds and heartache.

This is Los Angeles after all and if you haven't heard, L.A. has turned into an overdeveloped, overpopulated haven of starry-eyed babes hoping to be discovered. We're creatures of chemistry and are attracted to the physical and beauty, but that fades quicker than the film on the screen. You have the night of the living zombies roaming blind alone like robots in a futuristic war cartoon. They have all fallen into the cracks of the glitter. L.A. is a place of sandwiched in traffic with bad drivers polluted with foreigners and the occasional mousy woman slinking at a snail rate without any care or observation of those around them. It's the place of the Hollywood mogul fakes and phonies hideous on the outside, but living in gold. If any of them have anything in common with one another, it's there's nothing between their ears except air and madness with a tone of anger built up full of resentment. L.A. is a place of relationship fiction and friction ending abruptly without warning. Here you have a city that is about looks and about attractiveness, but when you look deeper, all you have is uncertainty. In L.A. if you've lasted in a relationship for four years and it ends you say, "Oh, we had a good run.", like its 'The O.C.' or 'C.S.I.'

Troy

Jagger met up with his buddy Troy and they headed down to the music store on foot. Troy is a preppy guy wearing his buttoned up dark pressed shirt, with the fancy tie dangling loosely around his neck by just enough so that his shirt can stay open at the top. Looking hot and dapper at twenty-two with blonde hair and brown eyes. He has very high ideals about commitment for a younger person. Troy views Jagger as his big brother, even though Jagger doesn't always feel grown up.

Jagger and Troy carouse up and down the music aisles scouring through the assortment CD compilations. Jagger wants to stock up on his chill out set to take him to a different place of inspiration to get his sex columns in order. He finds a love song CD box set that he pulls out to examine. He tells Troy, "Its three-discs and forty songs. I'm going to buy this, a bottle of wine and a razor blade. I'm buying shit. That's what people do when they're trying to push their emotions down. They drink, do drugs or buy crap they don't need."

Troy laughs reaching over to look at it.

Love is a complicated substance. If all we want is to get close, then why does one person pull away when the other person reveals any sign of interest? The second you stop showing interest they fly up your nose suddenly wanting your attention.

People are passionate when they are sexually stimulated. When they enter a relationship they slowly begin to lose the passion because they were only interested in the new experience. It's the fantasy of obtaining that object of desire. We are objects to many now aren't we? Once the object of your craving is in your hands you become fed up after a few rides and need an e-ticket to ride an entirely different roller coaster.

Jagger and Troy walk through one of the department stores to get back onto the promenade. On their excursion they pass the bedroom section where an enormous array of pillows adorn the aisles. Troy eyes the body pillows picking one up and holding it to his body, "I need to get me one of these."

Jagger eyes the pillows, "Bed feeling a little empty these days?"

"Yeah, and because it's been so hot out the last couple nights I've had to sleep on top of my covers naked. Luther, that dog I've been watching for a couple days climbed on top of me the other night when I was asleep."

"Okay, you know what? We need to get you a man and fast." Jagger pulls one of the pillows out, "I don't know if I could buy one of these out in the open. It would feel as shameful as renting a porno film. Can you imagine going up to the counter with one of these? 'Uh yeah, hi, it's for my friend, I mean my brother.'"

Troy laughs, "I have a question. In your dating rules, what date do you have the first good night kiss?"

"The first kiss should be short and sweet, no tongue and maybe have it at the opening of the date, that way at the end of the date it will be natural and longer."

"What do you mean natural? What date would this be on?"

"If it's on the first date, then by this point you better have not only had a conversation with him, but you've also already met him. If you are meeting him for the first time in person, then that is not a date. The kiss should be natural, easy and confident. Your lips are warm, relaxed, and for fuck sake keep your mouth closed. A classy kiss hello should not be out of the question."

How Jagger met Troy was an event in itself. It was a couple of hours outside of Los Angeles in a desert city. Jagger went to visit the city and stay there for a few days to attend a big weekend concert event that raised money for children in need of medical care. It was the first night of the concert where he met Troy who was seventeen at the time and enduring sick abuse at his parent's house. Jagger's seat was next to Troy's at the concert and the two of them hit it off talking for hours. Troy was enamored with Jagger's visible strength and wished he could be that confident. Troy showed him around the desert town the next day. He gave him a little tour while they got to know each other. Jagger was the first person he could trust in a long time. He didn't want him to go back to L.A. He felt safe while he was around. By the mid-afternoon, he told him about his life and how trapped he felt. Jagger was in horror listening to the stories. Anger oozed through him, but he remained serene like an immovable rock.

Troy came out and announced his sexuality in his early teens. His parents thought maybe they could beat it out of him. The beatings had already been persisting on, but they grew after the announcement. Whenever anything would go wrong he would be told it was his fault. He lost friends and support. People talked in smaller towns. He had to undergo the ridicule and harassment. He was a straight-A student and his grades began to waver. Feeling useless led him to have suicidal thoughts as a way out of his personal Hell.

Jagger and Troy decided to have dinner, but stopped by Troy's parent's house so that he could grab some extra things. Jagger waited in the car for what felt like an hour. He hopped out and paced back and forth in front of it.

In the house was another set up going on. "You're pathetic." His father said knocking Troy down not realizing Jagger had appeared on the porch. Jagger's head lowered with red in his eyes.

Everyone in the house jumped when the glass from the door made a loud crashing sound breaking into a million pieces all over the living room floor. One boot slammed onto the glass. Jagger was untouched and excessively fast for anyone to see what had broken in.

Troy's father charged over to Jagger, but it was too late Jagger's fist hit his face, "You fight him. You fight me first." The father was knocked to the floor. The mom grabbed the doorframe from the kitchen to the living room, "Please!"

Jagger was unresponsive by the pain he caused. "You should be ashamed of yourselves." His blood pressure barely rose when he spoke. He lowered to the floor like a terminator machine. He was swift, yet delicate when he grabbed Troy's hand to pull him up. Troy's body was wounded and he was unsure of what hit him. The mother was afraid to move. The father slowly tried to get up, but felt the sting of the attack.

Jagger said, "Say your goodbye's. He's coming with me. At least he'll be safe."

Troy looked up at Jagger and a smile formed. A real angel had swooped in to bring him to salvation.

"Let's get out of here."

In the car, Troy kept looking at Jagger idolizing him, fearing him, loving him and respecting him. He was scared not knowing where his life was headed, but at least he felt in protected hands and loved. A new sense of freedom and immense possibility overtook him.

"You can stay with me as long as you want." Jagger said with a relaxing voice.

"What if I can't find a place?"

"Then I guess you'll have to stay with me forever then." Jagger formed a rare smile that was full of warmth. This was another side of him Troy loves. He knows that Jagger is not all bad.

"My place is average sized, but it's comfortable and near the beach. There is a tiny studio guest home out back. You can stay there. Take all the time you need to figure things out."

Troy finished his remaining months at the high school near Jagger and enrolled in college. He's majoring in business with a minor in art history.

Troy spent the following year growing into his body, working out, and becoming quite a looker. His obsession grows a little too much on the exterior, thumbing through hot fashion magazines and sports magazines. He became privy to reading up on the gossip and nearly basing his existence on it. This is what happens to people that come from a smaller town or outskirt and move to Los Angeles. They focus in on the showiness becoming attracted to it. Luckily, he has Jagger around who makes sure he doesn't fall too deep into superficiality.

Slade

Jagger lies in bed asleep when his eyes shoot open as if possessed. His body rises abruptly as if he is a wolf. He moves into a crouched position like a cobra before planting both feet on the floor. Ready to attack from the moment his eyes open. Climbing out of bed he stretches his near bare-naked body. His tan toned shape forms into muscle as he reaches his hands up clasping them together. His boxers hang over his ass comfortably. They are pulled down slightly with reveal when he extends in a cat like stretch.

He shuffles around the room slow as if wounded. His feet kick up some torn blue jeans off the floor and he puts them on. This is followed by a tattered old T-shirt and then some flip-flops. He grabs his keys by the front door and picks up the pace outside. All in his way will be crushed if they don't jump aside. He doesn't care and it shows. He moves with purpose and discipline down the street to the local coffee and tea house on the corner of the block. Inside he picks up some Green tea and skims a nearby paper when one of those model-looking boys walks in hoping to be seen. When the model boy makes a move he poses while sucking in his cheeks and pursing his lips. Lucky for Jagger the guy decided to pick him to sit next to and expound on himself. The model boy's whole life story is put there on a platter for Jagger to savor. The guy grew up outside of Pittsburgh and went to college to study vocal performance in Iowa. This of course led him to move to overcrowded and pointless Hollywood to accomplish his dreams of stardom that will ultimately end in disappointment.

Jagger nodded attempting to be respectful even though his eyes were pasted to his paper. He cut in and out of what the guy was saying while catching himself from yawning out of boredom. Drifting off to a faraway place as the model boy's story grew fainter fading into the background. Jagger jolted back to reality in the middle of the guy's story and his mind tried to fill in quick what had happened. He knew he didn't miss much anyway. The model does whatever it takes morally to get his face seen and remembered.

"I'm always on model shoots, casting calls and meetings with Producers." He explained this to the wall with his head up high. Jagger could swear he had a light base of make-up on ready for his close up.

"Fame as your only goal is pretty hollow, but good luck." Jagger explains as his phone beeps with a voice mail. He checks it as the model continues to ramble on.

It's his buddy Slade on his voicemail:

"Jagger! It's eleven o'clock, take that fucking cock out of your tight ass and call me back. You're not home and I'm on your street. Where the hell are you?"

Jagger sends him a text message letting him know where he is.

Slade struts into the coffee shop sporting his signature wide smile. Men and women look up in awe from their newspapers, magazines and laptops undressing him with their eyes. He's damn hot and he knows it eating it up. His body is amazing and supple. He's a six-foot one muscular Adonis at twenty-eight. Slade is Jagger's sex-crazed fiend of a friend who eats and breathes sex and nothing else. He loves sex with many people and many at the same time. Sometimes he brags about some of the amateur porn he did for money he didn't need in his early twenties. As the counter opposite of Jagger, it's amazing that they connected at all. Jagger has high standards when it comes to relationships while Slade lives with a severe distaste for being tied down to anyone.

"Man!" Slade shouts with exuberance. He struts over to Jagger putting his arm around him.

"Thank God you're here." Jagger says low feeling saved.

"You're going to have to get used to this bud!" Slade shouts with mass extroversion wrapping his arm tight around Jagger as they leave the place.

Slade rubs Jagger's shoulder with one hand while they walk, "What's up with that man you call Heaven?"

"Hmm, Garth? You mean that guy that I follow around like a fucking idiot who wouldn't be caught dead anywhere near me?"

Slade smirks, "That would be the one."

"He doesn't know I exist and I can't find a way to say anything to him. You should see the way he watches me though. It reminds me of those old classic movies where

16

the girl would gaze on at the guy in the distance. It's hot. No one does that anymore. I wish I could touch him and know what that feels like. I want to know what it's like to sit next to him and feel his breath, to have the opportunity to gaze into his eyes and watch his smile. I want to feel what it's like to wrap my arm around him and grab his hand. Fuck man!" Jagger says smiling totally smitten in dreamland.

"Aww." Slade's lips move into hit Jagger's forehead. The wind blows through Slade's beautiful slightly spiked black hair. "If you talk like that I'm going to have to tackle you to the ground and take advantage."

"I'll win. We both know that."

Slade grabs Jagger's side with his hands giving it a tender squeeze.

Jagger brushes it off unaffected. "Garth seems like the type that would be happy to settle down with someone and have a family. Man, I'm crushing on him. Even if it doesn't happen I'm going to do it one day. I'm going to have a couple of kids. I don't know when, maybe in ten years who knows. I'll do it myself with or without someone."

"You're serious? You want kids?" Slade asks with revulsion. "Why?" This is unimaginable to him. His longest relationship with someone these days lasts four hours and that's more than fine with him.

"If I can save a child or two by adopting, and give them a loving place to grow up in then that is one soul I've helped on this planet in this lifetime. When you have a child your focus is on them and the people they're going to be when they grow up. It takes you away from your extreme narcissistic existence. Why not create an even bigger family. I have you, Troy and Russell. And that's all awesome, but why not expand this unit more?"

Slade smiles grabbing a leaf that falls through the air over them, "You'd make a great Dad! You'd be one of those hot Dad's I'd like to fuck."

Jagger knows he can count on him to be the voice of reasoning.

"There are some positives to being in a relationship, you know." Jagger pokes at Slade's sudden disdain over the idea of companionship. "I want to be part of my own self-created family unit. It's lonely having to make all the decisions in my life alone. I want to share myself and my life with another person in a committed relationship."

"You can make decisions with me." Slade offers.

"I want to be able to sleep with the person I'm making those decisions with." Jagger adds.

"We can do that too!" Slade jumps gleefully.

Two men walk past them with two boys trailing behind them. The two boys are each walking a dog. Slade leans into Jagger's ear. "Noah's Ark."

Jagger cracks a rare smile. "They can hear you."

"Good!" Slade laughs.

Slade is a non-deceitful honest player. The player in him began as a teenager. He knew he could get his fair share of whatever he wanted. His friend's mothers and even some of their fathers would see this kid and say, "Fuck this guy's hot and if we fucked just once, my universe would be rocked for eternity." Others would catch his eye and mumble, "Hang on to that one until he's eighteen, then let him nail me."

When Slade was twenty, he became a male stripper. He certainly didn't do it for the money. He was born into money and doesn't have to work a day in his life if he doesn't want to. The stripping was done for the excitement and rush of it. It was an adventure that satisfied his need to be worshipped and adored. Sometimes after the show he and some of the guys and girls would all get wild and have rowdy orgy sessions late into the night.

Slade did have a relationship at one point, but he had to end it. He suffocated and got strangled within it knowing quickly that it wasn't for him. There was no interest in ever going back into it again. He moved on up in the stripper world and started his own private business where he offered private party dancing sessions on call. You could book him for the right price. He loved being able to explore this naughty and thrill-seeking side of himself.

Are you a steamy hot boy or sexy play girl thing out for good times? Then you could be his playmate, but don't ever look for a ring to be put on your finger. He became a hot world-class playboy, not a good boy. He's been having fun ever since.

Slade isn't dishonest about who he is. He's up front and unapologetic about it. Because of this Jagger cuts him some slack. There is no misleading a guy emotionally. He is direct from the get go so they know immediately where he stands. It's clear he wants lots of sex and zero connections. His view is quite different from Jagger's, but they do agree on one thing and that is the open relationship terminology is a cop out. "What's the point?" Slade will say.

Those who are in true and genuine sex jobs typically feel the same way Jagger discovered in his research. You call it what it really is, *friends with benefits.* When you call it an open relationship you diminish the validity, strength, love and commitment of relationships in general. If you're incapable of being in an adult relationship without caving into pure animal instincts and adopting an adolescent attitude where anything is fair game, then don't be in a relationship. Psychologists and studies have shown that monogamous relationships are more stable than ones with either non-consensual adultery or consensual adultery. You may be having fun being in a relationship with three people, but it won't stand the test of time.

Jagger is used to subjecting himself to lower means in the name of research. One of the establishments was a sex club to interview the patrons that were discreetly sneaking in. He roamed around the dark seedy place with a notepad and pen stopping any random nudist to ask a few questions about themselves. On his way out he discovered Slade was following him. Jagger turned and shoved him back hard. "Can I help you?"

Slade formed a smirk and was immediately hooked in by Jagger's bold, little temper. He followed Jagger persistently down the street peppering him with questions until their dialogue between one another grew. Jagger's wall dissolved since Slade has that warm affect on people. They became simpatico and instant brothers and have been best buds ever since. Despite their differences on how relationships should be, Slade has been one of the closest mates Jagger has ever had. He has listened to the heartbreak in Jagger's voice after being fucked over by another cold fish that vanished without a trace after two dates. Slade drops the fine stud he's in the middle of fucking to be with his friend. He is sudden and present and it always rings in Jagger's ears. "I'm on my way. You can do better Jagger and you know it. He's not worth the trash in a garbage can." He'd hold the generally strong rock that falters from existence in those scenarios. Slade senses the inner compassion stirring up underneath Jagger's often insensitive outer core. Slade's unwavering loyal friendship seeps out of him, and that's why Jagger keeps him around.

Jagger did have some powerful interference stuff happening when he brought Troy to live with him. He forgot that Slade would eventually meet him. Slade would turn into a full time predator.

"Who is this boy you got living with you?" Slade asked with a sparkle in his eye.

"It's not like that." Jagger explained.

"Sure it isn't."

"It's not. Stay away from him." Jagger warned. "He's a good guy and doesn't need to be corrupted by you."

"And being close to you isn't going to corrupt him?"

"No, fucker."

"All I'm saying is let me have a taste that's all. Just an itty-bitty taste, let me have him," Slade's body simulates fucking as he gyrates in and out with his fist in the air, "Just once."

"Don't. You'll scare him. He's a friend of mine, which means he'll be your friend, like your brother. And you would never fuck your brother, would you?"

"Hmm, that's hot." Slade contemplates the vision.

"He's come from a bad place and I want him to feel welcome." Jagger informs him.

"Well, that's all I'm saying is that I'll make him feel welcome, really welcome." Slade shoots back.

Jagger narrows his eyes suspiciously, but he knows there is only so much he could do when it comes to Slade.

Slade did keep his word. Any initial physical attraction he had towards Troy faded quickly. He picked up a young drone to compensate for not being able to play with Troy.

Troy was too smart for that and turned off by hookups. This made the game way too hard for Slade. There are too many other dudes out there for him to play with. He couldn't be bothered with one he had to work to put out.

Slade insists that Jagger teeters from being a good boy and a bad boy and never knowing which side to stay on.

This fascinated him from day one. Their friendship grew at a slow and steady pace until they were inseparable. Both offered insight into what the other by nature didn't have.

Slade and Jagger head into the reception area at Jagger's Editor's office. Slade jumps onto a chair like a child and reaches for any old magazine. Ryan, the cute young male assistant catches Slade with a dreamy look in his eyes. Slade smiles at Ryan with heavy flirtation.

Jagger notices this, "Don't get into any trouble. I'll just be brief."

Slade doesn't break eye contact with Ryan. "Sure brother whatever."

Jagger shakes his head knowing what Slade is going to do.

Amanda is an Editor at L.A.'s trendiest and most popular magazines geared to the twenties and thirties set. She's a ball buster, strong, early 40's, long blonde hair and beautiful.

She sits down with Jagger, "How's my star columnist doing?"

"Why do you pick me to write about this relationship shit? I don't know what I'm doing half the time."

"People want to hear from a real person who experiences the same things they do rather than from someone who studied it from afar without diving into it firsthand. They want to hear what you have to say rather than some medical doctor." Amanda says eyeing Jagger's secondhand flip-flops.

"I've been a supporting player for so long." Jagger says soaking in her wisdom. "I know my point of view is just as valuable as anyone else's. You're right, it's about time for it to be heard."

"So what's the problem then?" She asks.

"It bothers me when I encounter people who see the world as black and white. My interest lies in the gray areas. I've come to the conclusion that it's pointless trying to enlighten others on matters that they can't comprehend."

"Those are the sorts of things I want you to share. Get me stuff like that for your next column. Why not talk about this little thing you got going on with your neighbor?"

Jagger is horrified. "What? My neighbor? Oh, no I'm not talking about this aussie lifeguard crush."

"You don't have to say it's about you, but there's something there. I think you should explore it. Just get it to me by the end of the week."

"Hmm. Well, I'll see what I can come up with that's safe."

"Never play it safe, Jagger. Those are your words remember?" She reminds him.

Jagger heads back out into the lobby and catches Slade leaning over Ryan's desk flirting. "Slade, let's go!"

Slade doesn't break eye contact with Ryan. "I'll call you."

Ryan is nervous and excited. "Okay."

Slade catches up with Jagger who has already bolted out of there.

Jagger forms a slight smirk. "Can't you just leave the help alone?"

"What the fuck. I'm just gonna borrow him for a night."

"Does he know that?"

Slade shoots a wide smile with devilish intent. "Hey you can have this with your Garth too if you say something to him."

"Oh no way. I'll get shot down. Although I had another prophetic dream about him that I hope comes true. In it, Garth approaches me to ask me out in a proper way. He holds all those qualities of a wistful medieval knight, courageous, tons of honor, and an immense amount of loyalty and consideration of others. We're together, the house, the white picket fence, the kids and the dog we call Blackhawk. Garth comes home from work and anxiously walks through the maze trying to find me so that we can embrace in love's everlasting kiss. We fall into each other's arms and onto the bed."

Russell

Russell is a thirty-six year old investor with matinee idol looks and dark brown hair that ruffles around like leaves in the wind over his beating brown eyes. He's always in complete command and control. He can get Jagger, Slade and Troy into most any restaurant or club that takes weeks to get reservations for. Racing in his show off Aston Martin into the valet driveway of an elite restaurant in Malibu, he steps out of his vehicle in his $2000 suit dripping with sexiness. He moves with haste ranting on his phone about some deal he's about to close. He is a tough guy and his face is downright stern, but what a smile when he lets one spread across his face.

"Yo, babe!" He leans over squeezing Jagger one.

"What's up?" Jagger asks ducking away from the crowd around the restaurant door.

"Man, I just closed a deal. This is it, another big one!"

"Look at you!"

"I know." Russell lets that smile spread wide again. "Come on. We're celebrating."

Russell is involved with Edward who is thirty-five. It's not exactly romantic bliss. They love screaming matches in public. Jagger pulled his truck up in front of their house one afternoon only to witness another lover's quarrel on display in the front yard. Edward was headed back into the house angry about misplacing his glasses again.

Russell shouted in a huff. "I'll fucking drive you then!"

Edward stomped up the stairs back to the house. "I'd rather drive blind!" It was a scene right out of Romeo & Juliet.

It was six years ago when Jagger met Russell. He was sitting at a bar alone after another bad dating scenario that fell apart after two weeks. Peeling the label off his beer bottle, a nervous habit he sometimes perfects, he didn't notice Russell there. Russell was sitting a couple of feet away from him ordering a drink at the bar. He was styling to the max, hair slicked back with dancing eyes. He saw the despair seeping off the elusive tough figure that sat before him.

"Man, I am totally digging you!" Russell's smile cracked open wide.

Jagger let out a melancholy sigh.

"Oh come on, what's a handsome guy like you down for?"

"It's been a long day. I mean: life. You're catching me at a very inopportune time."

"Well, I can fix that." Russell said with confidence as if he were closing a deal, "How about what do you say, you, me, my place, lots of VERBAL conversation. If that's going to get you out of the slump you're in, then it's my duty to help."

Jagger sat up in his bar chair to get a good look at him. "Is my slump that obvious? I've never been good with hiding it."

"Come on, we all see it, you've got complete control and your owning this place. You're hiding the fact that something is wrong, but I can feel it off you. What is bringing you down?"

"Love. Again." He swings his head towards Russell.

"Ah, L'Amour. You're a romantic." He winks. "I like it. Maybe you could teach me a few tricks."

Jagger couldn't help, but be smitten over his charm. "I'm not this easy, but you've caught me in a vulnerable state. Plus I'm alone and dreadfully single. This isn't stopping you from taking advantage regardless I see."

They headed for a stroll around the block while Russell pulled it out of him. No not his cock, but his candor. Russell's world is different and more colorful than Jagger's. Jagger loves that a guy is older than him for a change. He likes that he can lean on someone else if only for a minute. Being able to lean on someone who seems to understand him is rare in Jagger's world. Russell and Jagger ended up not consuming a sexual fling, but instead saw the beginnings of a friendship. They communicated into the night over a drink at Russell's place discovering their many similarities and values.

Russell had been through one annoying and depressing date after another, but he managed to stay optimistic. He was too good for all of his dates and needed someone of equal intellect, personality and looks. Although he and Jagger have always had a mutual attraction, it never seemed to blossom into more than a best friendship.

A business partner set up a blind date between Russell and Edward. Jagger was excited for Russell when he found out the guy has a PHD. "Oh good a doctor. You should see who he has been slumming around with lately. I mean the guys he goes out with ride around on skateboards. The date has to end early because they have curfew."

The possibilities of Jagger's friendships with Troy, Slade and Russell are endless. You can do no wrong in their eyes. It's nearly impossible to find great friendships like that with people who love you no matter what. They may sometimes find each other attractive and even sometimes joke about it, but when it came right down to it, they wouldn't go through with the deed out of respect. They all have something that is often seen lacking today and that is loyalty.

CHAPTER 2

Jagger's Early Years

Jagger cannot help fantasizing about fucking a chick one minute and fucking a dude the next. He is split right down the middle when it comes to his attraction to others. It's been this way since birth. Just as Freud once suggested that everyone is born bisexual. Human tampering and societal influences on the young child during the developmental phase mess with this natural innate quality. The mass majority of humans are easily led. They are programmed to roam through life like zombies. Everyone gets up in the morning at roughly the same time. They all head to work at the same time sitting in the same traffic jams. Most of them work the same amount of hours which is a full day, then they leave work to head back home exhausted around the same time. They have a good few hours left at night to have dinner, exercise and then not much else. This design is all man-made and taught and this is what life has become about.

Jagger teeters on that fine line between wanting both a man and a woman. If he's masturbating to a guy and that's not cutting it for him, sometimes midway through he'll fantasize that it's a woman he's fucking just to get off. It is not a mystery he wrestles with to understand. He leaves that for the gossip machines that are perpetually bored with their existence to wrestle with. There are moments where he questions if he's really attracted to men at all.

Jagger had this modest crush on two friends of his at the age of five. One was a girl and the other was a boy. It was his first glimpse of what his non-censored sexual preference would be like. His Don Juan-Casanova bone kicked into high gear from way back then. He lured them both separately into the open garage behind the apartment complex he resided at. What a little bitch. He didn't concern himself with privacy. He wanted to romance them one by one. The gigantic beat up Cadillac his parents shared was parked in the garage. This is where he stood facing the both of them. All three of them were friends and played together throughout the complex. They do what five year olds do. Ride their tricycles and play with trucks. Jagger leaned in and kissed each of them innocently. He leaned in and kissed the girl first. She had attitude and threw her hands up in the air angry. "Eww! Why did you do that!?" He hadn't perfected his language yet otherwise he would've retaliated. "Oh fucken' lighten up." He stood there short in height, yet debonair not understanding the attitude. Gee, wasn't expecting that. The less hostile boy smiled with a look on his face that said, 'that was pleasantly interesting'. Jagger was ferociously affectionate and it was his way of saying I like you. Nothing has diminished his steaming sexuality or inner passions that continue to burn bright. He hangs out in the vague grey area. He is clear about what he sees while others wade around the confusion district. His first boner was at age eight. This was when he discovered that you could stroke it too. This was also when he first masturbated to orgasm. It was the same year he started Catholic School and took his first communion.

THE HIGH SCHOOL EPISODE

Jagger turned his life into a whirlwind adventure as if he were in High School again. With Garth, he feels those rumblings that are as intense as they'll ever get at that age over a boy like Billy. High school was a place of many interesting memories for Jagger, most of which entailed he and his friends running around the city wreaking havoc. His relationship and sex advice started early, but instead of writing in notepads or in a laptop, he wrote in other places like the boys restroom. While in there with his friends he would write on the wall in big letters above the urinals: '*If you shake it more than three times you're playing with it.*'

At sixteen, Jagger wasn't always love-y dove-y either. He found other ways to further his sexual exploration. He loved the girls that wore skimpy clothing and who put on a play for him. The girls would flip their hair around and gaze at him coyly when he'd walk by. They'd beg him to pin them against the walls on the outskirts of the school during and after class. His boy crushes were more specific, always the same type of boys that interested him on a physical level. There weren't that many of them. It was one at a time while the girls remained on a plentiful basis.

He wanted to know the feeling of having a guy's warm mouth around his cock to give him a different meaning to the words: *Wake up and smile.* It's not a self-centered wish to have a guy woken up with a blowjob. More should give him the surprise instead of just little love notes. One of the best jobs you can do is when you alternate flicking your tongue against the tip of his cock with taking it completely in your mouth. The sensation is powerful and all you experience are fireworks.

Jagger's crush on Billy was a daily dream occurrence. One afternoon he took matters into his own hands to get Billy to notice him. He attempted his primal flirtation event at his locker during recess. He reached up to his locker allowing his shirt to lift up so Billy could catch a glimpse of his naked skin. Billy's blue eyes were raving with hunger staring at Jagger from across the way with drool hanging out of his mouth. Jagger could tell he was into him when he saw the fire burning in his eyes. Billy thought about the metal of the locker close to Jagger's body and he wanted that metal to be him.

Jagger's mind raced when Billy stood next to him. Billy looked good in his shirt. The material gripped his body in all the right places. His jeans were shaped to increase and emphasize that soft bulge between his legs.

He noticed Billy's *section* was no longer soft, but grew hard, bigger and swelling into a bulge. Jagger saw their flirtation had been going on unnoticed by the rest of the students. He walked away and Billy jogged up next to him.

"Hey." Billy motioned for him to follow him. Jagger's heart pounded uncontrollably as they slipped into the gym and into the boy's locker room. It was empty. In the back stood a place where they kept all the basketballs and other equipment. They knew it would be dark and private.

They followed each other in there and stood staring at each other. Jagger noticed Billy trembling and that made him more into him. Billy's muscles were tight, and he had an intense look on his face. Both were nervous as it would be their first time with another guy. Jagger could barely make out his blue eyes. He reached his hands out and they were stopped by Billy's stomach tight under his shirt. Billy grabbed his arm almost to stop it from happening out of guilt, but let his hormones take over.

31

Jagger let his hand drift traveling around every inch of the guy. He felt Billy's cock. It was incredibly hard. He was sure it was hurting him. His heart pounded feeling the thickness for the first time on another guy.

Billy unbuttoned and slowly unzipped his pants. He put his hands on Jagger, gesturing that it's okay to go ahead and explore him. He pushed Jagger's face into his crotch in a rough, but loving way.

Jagger pulled Billy's pants down and saw the head of Billy's cock flinching and poking out of his boxers a little. He pulled Billy's boxers down and his cock came out with force hitting him in the face. Jagger opened his mouth dying to know what it tasted and felt like. He put his mouth around the head of Billy's cock. Billy's cock slid into Jagger's mouth as far as he could take it. He could feel the thickness in his mouth and tasted how good the guy was. He put his hands around Billy's ass, rock hard in his jeans. He gave it a feel gliding his hands up and down his back and then down over his ass keeping it there. Before he could pull back he felt his cock swell and Billy's orgasmic gasp. Billy's cock slid back out of Jagger's mouth and it contracted and pumped cum on the floor. Billy's fingers dug into Jagger's scalp hard that it nearly hurt him as he took those powerful, rhythmic, hot, spurting loads and landing in succession. Billy reached over, pulled Jagger up, and kissed him on the lips.

NATASHA: THE ESCORT CHICK

Natasha was twenty-two when Jagger was seventeen. This was one year after his lust filled crush on Billy came true. He and Natasha had a hot and steamy affair that lingered for almost two years. She was a call girl for an escort service, but Jagger was too immature to care all that much. He was head over heels for her. They were both equally sexual and didn't mind swinging or fantasizing about those within their own gender. Natasha loved to drag Jagger to the strip clubs. It was more sexual energy for him to devour. She would get off on it too! He was in his own element. They'd watch the hot women dance and spin around the poles with vivacious eroticism. The girls would tear their tops off and their breasts would pop out lusciously towards the horny clients. It was the art of it Jagger loved, even though he was itching to lick and fondle their breasts. Men and some women sat alone watching the stripper dancers with their mouths open inviting it all in. Jagger and Natasha held hands near the stage while two of the girls stood on the platform above them. The strippers were excited to give them a private show.

In a dark nightclub with colored lights flashing, an eighties dance song plays while Jagger nods to the music as if he is James Dean cool. Bob, an older gentleman in his early sixties approaches him and whispers something in his ear. "You ever fuck older men?" Jagger's eyes are closed as he bobs to the music. He opens them coldly forward away from Bob.

"Sometimes." Jagger whips around facing the guy with his finger pointing hard into the man's chest. "For the right price."

Bob is a little frightened. He expected a dumb pushover guy, but instead was faced with something stronger. Natasha approaches them out of the dark with her tits falling out of her tight dress. She wraps her arm around Jagger. "What's going on here Jagger?"

Bob doesn't know what to think about them both.

Later, in a hotel room, Bob sits in a chair stroking his cock. He watches Jagger fuck Natasha hard on the bed in front of him. Not quite what Bob had in mind, but getting to see Jagger naked and in action is better than not having him at all.

At home, the sexual duo would get playfully aggressive with one another. Natasha would throw Jagger against the wall and his cock would grow hard with excitement. She would slam her body against his while they kissed intensely. She wore a thin shirt with no bra and he could see her nipples poking through it. He couldn't keep his eyes off them. His hands moved underneath her shirt lifting it up, ripping it off and watching her breasts fall out. Jagger would pull her against him with her tits pressed firmly on his carved out chest. Loving the way it felt he'd rip her shirt off himself. He'd watch her breasts come falling out each time in plain view for him to take into his mouth. She loved doing the same to him, watching his huge, thick cock popping out of his boxers. She would glide her hands delicately over his penis, sliding to the tip and back down again.

In between breaths of kisses all over her body he would whisper, "I found your underwear under the covers of my bed after you left the other night. What exactly did you want me to do with it?" Holding his cock in her hand, she inserted it into her clit. She pulled his body closer against her so she could feel all of him. This sent him in a hot frenzy. He lifted her up on him and his cock would move deeper into her. She could feel his balls slamming against her while he fucked her in and out.

They moved onto the bed and she climbed on top of him, moving her body so her tits would glide over his lips. He had to lift his head slightly to kiss and suck on them. As he kissed her, she grabbed one of his fingers and slammed it inside her. He went crazy with all the wetness while she cried out. He loved Natasha because she was the kind of girl that was insanely hot. She was all over the board when it came to sexuality. She'd have no problem doing it in an elevator, outside or in places where they could potentially be caught. Always naked and fooling around, he couldn't be with anyone who wasn't up for that regular task.

They were at it like clockwork every morning. Jagger would get up and push Natasha on her back. He would crawl over her like a god. She'd yank his boxers down and watch his cock pop out and feel his ass. Her wet pussy opened up even further. He moved in slowly making her wait by pushing in a little bit at a time teasing her. With a sudden thrust he'd slam his whole body into her. She moaned loudly feeling his hugeness grow even more inside her. She felt his cock slide all the way in until his balls were up against her. She gripped his arms and wrapped her legs around his ass while he fucked her hard. Just as he was about to cum, she clenched her pelvic muscles and he pulled out exploding in hot wetness all over her. She cried out lathering it all over her body and her tits. She wanted to feel all of him on her.

There were other times that she would close her legs instead of spreading them so that her pussy would be tighter for him. Sometimes she would climb on top of him and lie back a little. This way he could watch her move up and down on him and stare at her breasts at the same time. She would clench her pussy muscles so her inner walls would firmly grip his cock.

They joined two other girls once and went at it together swapping partners. Jagger being the only guy got the opportunity to fuck each one of them in front of the other waiting two. They all got a chance to feel him. He wanted to do his duty as a guy. He was open with her about wanting both a girlfriend and a boyfriend to go home to every night and to have the opportunity to wake up between them.

All good things end eventually and Jagger walked away from Natasha when he found out she was pregnant by an ex-boyfriend. His pride had been hurt and he knew things would never be the same between them. He looked back on it for what it was, just another fun, sexual experience that opened him up to a world that was ready to give him more. Jagger would remain Natasha's favorite and best fuck.

CHAPTER 3

The Drug Conquest

Jagger's had a gun pointed to him four times. Only one wasn't in an attempt to threaten murder. He was a former delinquent and a rebel. When that happens, then you become attracted to anything dangerous and often times come into the presence of drugs, convicts, hookers, hustlers and other outside outcasts. The gun was another ex-convict sitting on the couch at the home of the center of the drug world in the city of Hollywood.

Jagger sat on a couch opposite one of the ex-convicts recently released from prison. He had his feet up on the armrest talking to the ex-con. He had no concern and seemed oblivious to the pistol the man fondled occasionally aiming it at him during the conversation without intent to harm. The guy explained that he did kill some people and that he has no regrets. It was all over drugs and money, which makes it that much better.

How Jagger ended up there was no secret. It was through the guy who would soon become his ex-boyfriend, Reed. Reed introduced him to the seedier side of life. Reed was five years older than Jagger and was the guy everyone went to for the drugs. Jagger didn't know what Reed did for the first month after he met him. Reed was dealing at the college he went to. They had a class together and would discreetly watch one another enamored. Jagger had never done drugs and didn't know the signs of a dealer. Reed would walk around campus acting tough with his shirt off. There was always a crowd of admirers around him. There was something dangerous about him and Jagger was attracted to that at the time. He wanted him and could not shake that off.

Once when Jagger arrived at the school, some of the students were all sitting in front of one of the classes waiting for the instructor to get there and open the door. One by one they all said, "Hi Jagger." Reed followed behind them all with a smile. "Hi Jagger."

Jagger was covered in sunglasses and glanced up with rough aloofness noticing that Reed spoke to him. "Hi."

It was the first time they had any verbal interaction. Reed continued to watch him as he walked into the classroom.

When June rolled around and the school year was over, they both knew it was now or never. There was a big party at one of the student's parents houses blocks away from the campus. Jagger noticed Reed was there. He stopped talking to one of the guy's mid-sentence and walked towards him. He fought his way through the crowd to the circle of people that were around Reed. Jagger knew he was going to flirt with him big time. Nothing and no one was going to stop him.

At the end of the night, Jagger discovered that a group of the party goers were hot for Reed as well. They were all fighting like wildcats to get with him. Jagger scoffed and walked away. "Fuck this shit. You can have him."

Reed took notice of the one that walked away, so naturally that was the guy he wanted. Reed watched Jagger with a smile and followed him. "Hey Jagger, can I take you home?"

Jagger was caught off guard for a moment knowing that he didn't need to be taken home. "Uh, yeah sure." Jagger figured he'll find another way to get back to his car.

Reed tried to feel Jagger out as they headed to Reed's car. He didn't know which way he swung as far as sexuality goes. He didn't want to make the wrong assumption. Jagger assured him at that point. "Don't worry you're on the right track with me. I'm not picky, I eat what you put in front of me."

"Whoa-okay." Reed laughed liking it. He intended to bring Jagger over to his place. It was the first time Jagger went all the way with another guy since Billy. They fucked and played with each other sexually for about four hours. It was put up there on the list of some of the best sex they ever had. Reed asked if he could have his number.

Jagger said, "What for?"

Reed was offended, but he wrote his number on a piece of paper for Jagger anyway. "Call me if you want to."

Reed dropped Jagger off back at his car where the party was the next morning. When Jagger arrived at home he threw Reed's number in the trash and then proceeded to vomit. He couldn't believe what he did with another guy.

Over the course of the next three weeks, Jagger couldn't stop thinking about him though. He fixated on his hot body and the danger element that plagued this guy's aura. His mind drifted off to that huge cock of Reed's. He couldn't contain himself any longer that he went on a mad hunt searching for his number while kicking himself for throwing it away. He called one student after another. They all referred him to someone else and so forth until Jagger finally found one person who had it. His intense passion for the guy was erupting.

He called Reed and left a message. He paced and waited hoping he would call him back. It had been three weeks since he was with Reed and therefore assumed he might have forgotten who he was. On the contrary, Reed grew horny and intoxicated by being pursued like that. He called Jagger back and asked him to go out on a proper date with him that night to the movies.

They started to see each other regularly, hanging out, going out, making out and fucking every other day. Reed had a strange night schedule and it was a month or so in when he told him about his drug business. Jagger was already attached to him and blew it off. "That's fine."

Reed kept the drugs sealed from Jagger as much as he could. He didn't want him near that world. He treasured and prized him. Jagger was also a possession to look good on his arm.

Six months into their relationship Jagger demanded that Reed let him try the cocaine. He was already smoking the marijuana so how bad could it be? After much resistance Reed folded and put some cocaine on a key showing him how to snort it. That was the beginning of the end. One line of coke led to another and so forth. Jagger loved the stinging feeling and the temporary alertness it granted him. It made him feel euphorically happy and even more sexual than usual. He loved the abundant energy he had and the bitter drip down his throat as it worked its magic. Only problem was that it was short lasting. He was soon off to consume in more drugs to sustain his new bad habit.

A year into the relationship, Jagger was living with Reed and strung out from the constant drug use. Things took a rough tumble downwards as the drugs were everywhere. People were always over at the house and Jagger was feeling more worn out from the constant partying. Reed was aloof, unemotional and disconnected from him. The relationship lacked passion and love. There was fucking, but that's all it was. Zero emotion or feeling involved. Jagger felt more like an object and grew bored with this charade.

Reed started using most of his own supply and kept getting arrested. Jagger would get collect calls in the middle of the night to bail him out of jail. This didn't seem to bother Jagger, but what did irritate him was Reed committed the ultimate betrayal in Jagger's eyes and that was the vow of their relationship. He found out a secret from a mutual friend while enjoying a beer and a line of coke on the phone with Dustin. Dustin was joking around and slipped in his annoyance of Reed's sex addictions and indiscretions.

Silence fell over Jagger as he wasn't sure if he heard right. "I'm sorry what?"

Dustin realized he fucked Reed over. The nature of his relationship was blown out into the open. "Oh shit. You didn't know?"

"No. I got to go, I...." Jagger hardened trying not to weaken.

"Oh man, I'm sorry I thought you knew. Please don't tell Reed you heard it from me."

"I got to go." Jagger hung up the phone and paced like a cougar before its attack. He ran his hand through his hair and eyed the beer bottle sitting in front him. He grabbed it smashing it against the wall. His eyes flooded with mist, but he refused to shed a tear. He wouldn't allow a guy to martyr him. No, it would be better to exact revenge.

He called Dustin back. "Can I come over? I don't feel okay."

Dustin opened the door. Jagger walked in sullen and defeated with his bag. It was a sign that he was intending to stay the night. They sat up and talked. He pressed

Dustin to tell him who the guy was. He wanted any and all information he had on him, besides the fact that he's sleeping with his boyfriend. Dustin obliged. He had been Reed's friend for a very long time, but after meeting Jagger he took a bigger liking to him over Reed. He had a secret crush on him as well which he hinted in hushed tones.

Sitting on the couch together, Jagger jumped up licking his chops. "That's it I'm out! This is how it is with guys? Fuck this shit! I'm going back to girls."

Dustin's eyes grew teary and overwhelmed by the aggression and hot intensity Jagger displayed. "If you leave, we're screwed. You're the only good one around."

"I'm sure I'm not and I don't care for that responsibility. Find somebody else." He grabbed his keys and headed out towards the door.

"Wait!" Dustin rushed up to him, "Stay here tonight. You shouldn't be home alone anyway." Jagger stood by the door with his head half cocked. Dustin massaged his shoulder, "You're too upset. I can help."

Jagger sat down on Dustin's bed somber and defeated. He knew what he was doing and although it didn't feel right, he was too lost to stop. Dustin moved in on him close and pulled him into the bed and wrapped his arms around him all night. It was the first time Jagger was held by another guy in an honest position. Reed didn't have an emotional bone in his body and only hugged him hello – if that. Jagger would hold Reed in bed when he was experiencing withdrawals and needed to latch onto something to come down from it. He figured he was doing his part as a concerned boyfriend. Dustin told Jagger that Reed was sexual with a guy named Jim and where to find him. And that was that.

The door opened at Jim's house. He was fifteen years older than Jagger. Jim was average, shady and not particularly attractive, but not unattractive. Jim was love-struck when he saw Jagger standing there.

"Hi, Jim?"

"Yeah." Jim ogled the ingenuous figure up and down and knew he hit the jackpot.

"I'm Jagger. I'm sure you've heard of me at one point or another."

Jim grew fearful after hearing his name. He knew that there might be trouble and that Jagger might be dangerous. Yet, he noticed Jagger to be more like a wounded animal at this point, but capable of pouncing if pushed.

"Why don't you come on in?" Jim asked.

Jagger walked in the house feeling out of his element and territory being on someone else's turf.

Jim shut the door. "Come in, relax, have a seat. Can I get you something to drink or do you want to do a line?"

"I'll have both." Jagger cut him off.

Jim nodded and was feeling hot and drawn to Jagger's bad boy loner youthful quality. He had never met someone in their early twenties who was that sure of themselves, while still appearing vulnerable and sweet at the same time.

"What kind of drink?" Jim asked.

"Gin & Tonic if you have it."

Jim put some cocaine on the table and Jagger immediately began processing it with a razor. Jim went into the kitchen to make Jagger's drink while he made his 7up and Vodka on ice. He came out with the drinks. Jagger snorted in the first line of coke. He closed his eyes with a slight grin on his face as he took it in. He anxiously opened and closed his legs in and out handing the straw to Jim while giving him a naughty smirk.

After an hour of talking, Jim leaned in and began to kiss Jagger who let it happen. He had never cheated on anyone and only saw it as a death sentence, but knew his relationship was crumbling anyway now that Reed's oath to it was long broken. The relationship no longer had any validity in his eyes since Reed took a step outside of it. Now Jagger's own foot was out the door.

Jim's tongue pushed its way into Jagger's mouth. He pulled Jagger's shirt off and kissed his chest, his pecs and down his body to his abs. Jagger looked away resentful and uninterested as Jim made his way down to his cock.

Jagger fucked Jim hard with anger as if he were punching him. Jagger was officially gone. When they awoke in the morning in the same bed together, Jagger asked Jim for a favor.

Jim grabbed the phone and dialed it. "Hey, Reed? What's going on?" Pause. "Oh yeah?"

Jagger's face showed no sign of emotion, but defeat and reflection. Silently without breaking his eye contact from off the floor he extended his arm and hand slow towards Jim.

"Yeah," Jim saw Jagger's hand and smiled, "Yeah right, hang on a sec. Someone here wants to talk to you." Jim handed the phone over to Jagger.

"Hey baby," Jagger's tone had vengeance that no more was needed to come out of his mouth. Reed knew what had happened from the tone. The real war was about to start.

Jagger formed a devious smile, like a mischievous child playing with matches. He handed the phone back to Jim without looking at him. "He hung up. It's going to get really good now."

"Whoo! You are bad." Jim laughed out loud.

The phone rang and Jim picked up. "Hello...yeah.... where?... Okay." He hung up and looked at Jagger. "He wants you to meet him over by Alvarado and Sunset."

"Undisclosed location. What a pussy. I'll be there. I know where he's really talking about."

"Do you want me to come with you?" He asked.

"No, it'll only make it worse than it already is."

Jagger's sweetness enveloped his dangerous exterior. When he gives you a look, it's a look that says he understands everything and you believe him. You know that he knows what he's talking about no matter how hard it comes out of his mouth.

Jagger's car pulled up at the spot that Reed requested. Reed was emptying out his own car with crap. It was junk he smashed in it from his tweaking high all night. He had his back turned away from Jagger. "I can't believe you Jagger!"

"Interesting and what about you?! So it's okay that you do it, but when I do it I'm the bad guy?"

"Yes! Yes! You are the bad guy!" Reed was high as a kite and so far gone on the cocaine that having a civil conversation would be impossible.

They moved into a vicious shouting match at one another in front of onlookers. When they'd run out of insults to hurl at each other, they resorted to physical violence shoving each other with anger. The fact that Reed cheated on him repeatedly wasn't enough. Jagger had to fend him off physically for getting back at him. Reed was strung out and every time he pushed him, Jagger's fist knocked him a hard right.

"Come on let's do this!" Jagger spit a bit of blood into the street.

They fought until they both wore themselves out. A neutral curb was found to sit on a few feet apart unable to look at each other.

Reed smoked his hundredth cigarette. "Look I know this isn't what you signed up for with me."

Anger bled off Jagger's body like poison.

Reed abruptly changed his tune and focus, which is typical of a Gemini. "I'm sorry I have no respect for Jim. It's you I respect."

Jagger scoffed sarcastically. "Yeah, I can feel your respect."

They managed to continue the deteriorating relationship for another seven months. The violence and drug abuse progressed in a rapid fashion spiraling into more chaos. Reed became more strung out and Jagger wondered if he ever knew the real Reed. He wanted to know who that person was and wished that was the guy he got to have instead of this deadbeat bitch. Jagger had enough and was fantasizing about getting rid of him, getting out and being single. He didn't want to do drugs anymore and wanted to stop. It was no longer any fun and nor was the relationship.

As Jagger attempted to use less of the drugs, this created even more friction, because neither he or Reed were on the same level anymore. One of them is sober and the other is not. He didn't trust Reed and didn't find walking away easy. He had a strong loyal commitment to his significant other through good times and bad. You stay together no matter what. Part of being in a relationship is work and endurance, not just wine and roses. There was no love and one person can't be the only one working at it. He was caught in a jam and didn't know the answer so he stayed. The option to walk did not exist even though the thoughts were growing in him. Jagger was experiencing tremendous growth at a rapid rate and Reed was staying in one place not changing or improving.

Instead of leaving, Jagger accompanied Reed in assuming an odd drug using friendship with Jim. One night they were wandering the streets at 2am high on cocaine. Reed walked away from Jagger and Jim to pretend to use his phone. Jim put his game on and flirted closely with Jagger by a tree in the dark. He turned around only to find Reed standing there seeing red.

"What the fuck do you think you're doing?!" He shoved Jim. "I purposely walked away to see what you would do!"

Jim pushed him. "Fuck man, we were just talking."

"I saw what you were doing, you were moving in on him!" Reed charged past Jagger. He rammed and threw Jim to the ground punching him. "You stay the fuck away from him!"

Jim pushed him off and then body slammed Reed against the tree. Reed's fist flew a punch that nearly scathed Jagger's face and successfully hit Jim. Jagger lost his balance and was thrown back into the dirt. He popped back up on his feet and took a step back. 'What is this shit?' Jagger charged in between them to break it up and got knocked down in the interim. He charged back over in between them one more time. "That's enough!"

Jim stormed off angry. "Fuck this." Reed got up and put his hand out to Jagger. "Let's go baby." Jagger deliberated shaking his head and then went along with him. Reed let off some steam venting verbally about what a creep Jim is. As his high took over, he led Jagger into another dark place surrounded by trees. He unzipped his pants and pulled his cock out for Jagger who rolled his eyes annoyed.

That night they fucked each other hard shoving the other against the wall. The one thing they had that was unanimously euphoric was their fucking. They could both go on for hours with their big sticks, but even that never lasted. Reed used more of his drug supply and was incredibly fucked up around the clock. The one-day a week that he was sober he would be getting into his best clothes to go out at midnight. He wouldn't be home until the next evening. Jagger knew he should've been climbing into bed with him if he was really into this relationship.

They fought every time Reed went out. "Where the fuck are you going tonight?" Jagger asked.

"Don't worry about it." Reed would say.

Reed would kiss him on the cheek goodbye with zero passion. He thought that would cut it for the young horny cute boy he had on his arm. Instead, Jagger would hold the pillow tight and do is best not to cry about it ever. Strong boys never cry. He let the pain die inside him instead. When you don't let it out, that pain grows and eventually unleashes a monster. It hits others in a billion different ways and in many forms.

Jagger had enough weeks after his twenty-fourth birthday. He and Reed got into another knock around fest that got bloody. Reed had become unusually good at starting fistfights. Jagger wondered if they were cut from the same cloth.

He bolted for the door, but Reed ran passed him to get to it quickly. He chained, bolted and then blocked it. Jagger knew there was no way out except to fight his way out.

After minutes of punching each other around, Jagger talked his way out of there. He knew Reed was too fucked up to know what was going on around him or what he was promising him. Those promises were merely to trick Reed into believing that Jagger is on his side. Jagger knew as soon as he escaped and sweet talked him out of there that they were finished. He had enough of Reed's ridiculous drama and issues.

Reed unlatched the door and Jagger smashed out of there. He knew how close to freedom he was if he could get to his car. Once he drove off he would be released.

The path from the front door down the hall to the car outside appeared light years away. It only stretched further as he walked quickly to it hoping Reed wouldn't change his mind and come outside after him. Jagger made it to his car trying to keep from trembling as he attempted to insert the key into the ignition to start the car. He rolled down the window as far as it would go when Reed's hand slammed down on top of it.

Jagger jumped.

"You're coming back right?" Reed said staring at him with the Devil in his eyes.

"Of course I am." Jagger knew he wasn't going to ever go back, but he couldn't say that or he'd never get out of there. He wouldn't let him see his inner panic.

Reed continued to back away slow studying him unsure if Jagger was telling the truth.

Jagger's foot hit the gas and he raced away as far away from him as he could. He hid out and seized his stuff when he knew he had an open window of safety. When Reed was out all night or passed out on the drugs was the best opportunity to enter his place.

Reed looked for Jagger, but fell so far down into the bell jar that he forgot what he was looking for and gave up. He became more strung out and lit every second. Jagger figured he was dead after hearing no word for some time.

When Jagger left him to clean up and straighten up his life, he made a three-month pit stop frequenting the main drug home for mere entertainment purposes. Perhaps it was to feed his hungry inquisitive mind, or maybe it was because they were as rough as he was and had become his family. It was all that or boredom. They all knew to keep Reed out or warn Jagger if Reed was in the area. They may have all been fucked up night owls, but they were loyal to Jagger and he appreciated that.

Jagger was using the drugs and drinking the hard liquor all night. He made himself more than useful and cut up the cocaine lines for the other users, chopping and dicing the white powdered form that was sitting on a cutting board in a small heap. If being with Reed had taught him anything, it was how to weigh and measure and cut properly for the other users. He couldn't stand how imprecise about it the rest were.

The drug home was run by the main empress woman, Chantal. She was about fifty years old and married to a member in the French embassy. She was Hollywood's drug lord prancing around her mansion in a G-string and tank top letting in hustlers, prostitutes and all felons to get drugs and hang out all night. It was the home where they could be accepted by their own kind. Each had their own story on how they got there. In a way, she was Jesus in how she accepted them. He admired that part of her, but that was about it.

By the third month, Jagger was growing bored with getting high and hanging with dope fiends with no purpose.

He continued to cut up the lines for the group that happened to be at the house one night without any intention of using the drugs anymore. He passed the white substance out as if they were pamphlets.

Chantal is about six feet tall with aging exotic looks. She was a former runway model in France in her twenties. Now she lives off her husband's money in Hollywood. Her husband is a conservative man who sits on the embassy chair in France unaware of his estranged spouse's bad habits or he's in denial.

She sat at the high seat in her string bikini while chain smoking her twentieth cigarette. With her low raspy French accent of a voice she gazed at Jagger lazily. "You are not having any?"

Jagger looked up at her with his perfected venom stare and continued cutting the coke up. "No, I'm done. I'm stopping. Not using anymore."

Chantal laughed an evil Jekyll outburst. "You can't stop."

Jagger detected that she was implying his will is not strong enough. "Oh yes I can and I have." He walked to the kitchen to do another shot of whisky from the huge jug that sat on the counter.

Hours passed and everyone was getting more tweaked out of it that they all suddenly looked ridiculous in Jagger's reality. He knew he would have to leave this. As much as he loved them he would have to end it completely and be detox free. He was finding that the drugs masked love. He couldn't thrive in the atmosphere if he stayed.

He walked up to Chantal who was swaying to the music. Her G-string rode up her ass as she glided over the sounds of the music with a cigarette dangling from her fingers.

"I'm leaving." Jagger's voice was assertive and to the point.

"Aghh!" Chantal let out an angry scream and whacked him with her cigarette. The burn seeped into the skin on his arm. Ordinarily he would've struck back, but knew she was too fucked up to realize what she did. She was falling into the abyss like Reed.

"I'll see ya." He made his way towards the front door.

She turned around shouting at an unimaginable decibel. "If you get off this spaceship don't ever think about getting back on!!"

"Man you are off your fucking rocker! This is not a space ship and you are not an alien!" He stopped at the kitchen near the front door.

She went on a rampage shouting at the top of her lungs, "GET OUT!!!! AGGHHH!!"

David, her twenty something boy of the month came jogging up to him. "You're leaving for good aren't you? Don't lie I know it." Jagger felt sympathy for him. He knew David didn't want him to leave him in this mess, but he can't save everybody. Right now he has to save himself.

Chantal continued to shout and scream incoherencies.

"Yes, I'm leaving. I have to. I'm through with this bullshit." He told him.

"Let me give you my number." David insisted.

"You can, but I'm not calling." Jagger was determined to leave it all behind even if some of them were good people. He had to rip them out of his life for good no matter what or he'd never move on and form a better world. Chantal's ominous gibberish continued in the background.

Jagger backed up and eyed the jug of whisky. He moved briskly grabbing it and bailing out of her private expensive condo with it. As he headed down the hall outside her condo he shoved a cigarette in his mouth and lit it. It was 1 a.m. when he walked into the elevator. It stopped on another floor and two polite Asian girls walked into the elevator dressed up. They looked over at him slightly nervous for a second. Jagger was quiet, tough and menacing with his eyebrows arched angrily and the cigarette dangling from his lips. The doors to the elevator closed. He saw a sign in front of him, 'NO SMOKING.' Shit. He noticed the girls and grumbled. "Sorry." His voice was low and gritty. The girls smiled uneasily that more or less told him it was okay. What else are they going to do anyway?

As the elevator reached the first floor he realized he forgot his keys at Chantal's. "Fuck!" He threw his head back pissed at himself.

The girls walked out of the elevator and he pressed the key to go all the way back up to Hell again. He cursed himself silently for forgetting his keys in that place.

The doors of the elevator opened for him and he marched out with such force he would've ended someone's life that got in his way. He was not to be fucked with.

Chantal's door was unlocked and he barged right in. She was still pacing and screaming he couldn't believe it. What a nut case! He eyed his keys on the counter, seized them and bailed out of there. No one noticed when he went in there with all the racket surrounding the place. He wanted to start laughing at how close he was. He bailed out of there. He was done with Chantal, done with Reed, done with all of them. He felt free. He got rid of all his vices, the drugs, the cigarettes, the partying all night. A complete turnaround of his life was made in the months to follow.

He thought he saw Reed with a shopping cart full of trash loading it into a car once, but he couldn't be sure.

Chantal's straight-laced twenty-five year old daughter made a surprise visit to her mother's condo. She was horrified at the sight of her mother. There was strange writing's all over the walls and her mother was officially in a mental institutional state. She stopped taking the medicine that kept her equilibrium in balance. The daughter called the husband and he took a flight out to Los Angeles to clean up the mess.

At one point when Chantal was cleaned up she attempted to track Jagger down a number of times to apologize and ask him to come back. He never responded as he meant it when he made the choice to cut them all out.

Six months later he was officially clean and re-emerged a brand new person with a new outlook. Everyone noticed his body, his looks, and his mind all grew more enhanced and better than ever. He developed into something of an unstoppable force and a well oiled toned machine. It felt better than all the chemicals he was putting into his body and all of the toxic people he had come across. He made a pact to never veer off this path again. He grew a solid bullshit detector that those around him sensed. His nightlife of insaneness was over. He didn't find what he was looking for. Instead he was fed up by the nonsense of it all. It no longer interested him. He was heading to a clearer and brighter, new world.

CHAPTER 4

The Vegas Stripper Club

Las Vegas is beautiful desert nights, warm winds, Steve Miller band blaring out of the speakers and cold beer. Sin City was the beginning of Jagger's lifelong friendship with Sage. His connection with Sage bloomed with basic common interests along with their similar temperaments. They were both born in the same year and are into the same things. Classic rock, the beach and the Vegas desert baby!

Sage is one of those super hot guys that will walk into a room with pompous arrogance and everyone including him knows he's the shit. Women love him. Men love him. He's not like Slade exactly, although there are certain physical similarities. The black hair, blue eyes and similar build bit. Slade is into guys, while Sage is into girls.

Sage is a buff guy, a genuine jock who loves his football Jersey's. He even plays the game once in awhile. He's the kind of guy who puts up cardboard cutout stands of his favorite sports players around his apartment. He loves women and has many admirers around him. He has a flavor every week in fact. After he initially grew close to Jagger he had an attraction to frequenting the gay clubs and bars. He would drag Jagger with him who ironically loves the sports bars, because he can chill without being gawked at, judged or bugged. It has nothing to do with bisexuality or bi-curious or secretly gay or any of the bullshit labels that gossip mongers sit around in circles analyzing to death so they can justify who they are in hopes of gaining comfort from it. Bisexuality is not all black and white because sexuality is not all black and white. Sage loves the gay bars and clubs for the energy, the freedom, and the confidence that isn't hidden away the way it is in the frat clubs. He has an Italian background and with that often comes a big cock!

Sage was dating Jacey who is one of Jagger's sisters. Jacey is a stripper/dancer. Her dating set up with Sage only lasted a month, but in that time Sage and Jagger became reacquainted. Jagger had worked with Sage a year before this, but he wasn't friends with him. Jagger, Sage and Jacey had no idea they were all connected somehow.

At twenty-five years old, Jagger had spent a year becoming a more intelligent being. He fixed himself up and loved his complete removal from his drug using relationship days with Reed over a year before.

Jacey had been dating Sage for a week when she called Jagger up. "Do you know who Sage is?"

"No." Jagger said. He did not remember that a year before he had worked with him.

"Well, he knows you!" She said.

"I don't know who that is."

"We were talking the other day and he said, '*Wait a minute, do you have a brother named Jagger?*'"

After her endless description of him, it dawned on him who Sage was. Jagger remembered the image of this hot looking guy who walked with a cool vibe to his step. He thought it bordered pretentious and obnoxious. Sage worked all the girls who swooned and competed for him. He was always hooking up with some girl at a party.

Jagger was turned off. "Oh okay. I remember him now. You know what, let me tell you something about Sage, he's so smooth that you guys will be finished before you start. He's with a different girl every other week."

A few days passed and Jacey called Jagger up again. "Sage wants you to come over for dinner."

Jagger sighed irritated and having no interest in seeing or talking to Sage. "No thanks."

"Come on it'll be fun. Becky is coming too. You like her. We can throw a little party together."

"Look, I'm not interested."

"He wants to see you." Jacey attempted again.

"Oh brother. What for?"

"Don't be a jerk." Jacey kept pressing until Jagger succumbed to the pressure, "Fine, what time?"

Jagger walked into Jacey's house to go toe to toe with Sage. Sage was hotter than before. He was buff, strong, muscular and quickly turned shy when Jagger appeared. His eyes dilated over him nervously. Jagger thought it was a different side of Sage he hadn't seen before. He shook his head and thought, *'Great he knows about my history. Thanks, Jacey.'*

Sage found Jagger secretly beautiful, yet all male. He was immediately comfortable with him. They both barely had to put in any effort to connect. It was a natural back and forth camaraderie. Much different than how Jagger originally remembered him a year before.

After Jagger and Sage had official get to know you polite chitchat, Becky arrived at the house and the real party began.

Becky is voluptuous, sensual, and sexual. She and her longtime boyfriend have porn out all over their apartment. Adult Magazines and DVD's piled sky high in every corner. Jagger was Becky's friend for a bit and when he had enough of her antics he walked away. She conveniently moved into Jacey's life after that. Jagger saw it as a lousy attempt to get close to him. Years passed and both made their peace with it. Neither of them brings it up.

After Becky arrived, the girls went to smoke on the balcony. Jagger cranked up his Classic Rock music, which included Fleetwood Mac and the Eagles rotating at a high decibel out of the speakers.

"No fucking way man! I love this too!" Sage smiled from ear to ear heading over to Jagger to hi-five him. Jagger was stunned that he was finding himself warming up to Sage. He never could have guessed that would happen in a million years.

Sage shouted, "Come on man let's do some Vodka shots." They went into the kitchen and Sage pulled out the bottle and began pouring.

"1-2-3." They clinked glasses and shot it.

The good buzz seeped in and they did another one before they got unmanageably crazy. The girls took a break from their cigarettes to run inside to grab shots as well.

Jagger entertained Sage expounding on juicy mini-plots with his stories. The look in Sage's eye was one of passion and glimmer. He sat back on the couch not able to keep his eyes off Jagger who was sitting on the floor near him. Sage wanted to hear more beautiful words out of his mouth. He was secretly drawn to him in a deep friendship way and couldn't help fantasizing about him a bit. If he weren't into girls he'd be falling in love with him. He knew that much. *Why can't Jagger be a girl?* Sage thought. He would marry him on the spot.

The buzz overtook Jagger after several hours. He crawled on the floor in the middle of his story and went to sleep under the coffee table. Sage was dumbfounded, amused and attracted at the same time. He couldn't help himself or his thoughts.

When Jagger woke up the next morning, he was in his sister's spare room asleep.

Messages abound on his cell phone.

He called his sister back who was out at the strip club rehearsing and hanging out with her dancing gal pals.

"Wanted to make sure you were okay sleepyhead. Sage was worried and he's been calling me all morning to check up on you."

Jagger scratched his forehead. Why would Sage give a shit?

"He carried you to the bedroom!" She said.

"What? Oh geez." Jagger grows slightly embarrassed by the image coupled with some admiration. This guy cares about him.

"He wants to see you again. He really likes you. He was saying, 'damn, your brother is amazing! He has so much personality! I genuinely want to get to know him.'"

Jagger wondered why it sounded like they had been on a date. He mumbled, "I liked him too."

"Good because he wants to go to Vegas and wants you to come with us. It'll be the four of us. You, me, Sage and Becky."

"Oh god. I don't know. I don't think so."

Jacey urged and pleaded, but Jagger didn't budge.

Sage asked Jacey for Jagger's phone number so that he could begin the process of working him. He was determined to do whatever it took to get Jagger to come with them. He courted Jagger's own buddies for advice on how to convince him. One of those friends explained to Sage on how it is. "Jagger does this. It can be like running into a wall with him sometimes, but he'll go. Just keep pressing him. Don't back down and he'll come around. He'll realize your interest is solid and it'll speak volumes of your character."

Sage didn't back down. He kept on until the night before they were to drive to Vegas. Jagger pulled up at Sage's place with his bags without a word.

"YES! Man!" Sage laughed excited like a happy kid. He barged out of his apartment and jumped over the stairwell. He jogged up to Jagger and gave him a big, tight hug. Jagger chuckled thrown off by the exuberance, but turned on by it too.

The girls sat in the front seat driving everyone through the desert of California to Vegas. Jagger and Sage sat in the back seat talking each other up the entire way like two close brothers. The more Jagger spoke, the more fondness Sage grew for him.

In Las Vegas, Sage taught Jagger how to play blackjack so he could win some serious money. Jagger became hooked on the game. This went on all night until about 3:30 in the morning when all four caught up with each other in the busy casino on the downtown strip. They went outside and passed a strip club which made Jacey excited. "Let's check it out!"

All four of them walked into the dark strip club with the music pounding in their chests. It grew louder as they worked their way in to the place owning it. The stage lights were focused on a couple of hot looking girls with their tops off. They spun around on poles in their own occupied territory. They were sexy beautiful Angelina Jolie voluptuous type girls. Jagger and Sage both had growing boners watching their bouncing tits in the patron's faces.

Sage and Jagger sat in their own little booth big enough for two. Jacey and Becky walked past six empty booths and sat further away from the boys. A cocktail waitress named Daisy walked up to Jagger and Sage with a couple drinks. "Hey boys, how would you like one of these girls to take you in the back alone and give you a private lap dance?"

Sage laughed self-consciously becoming snowed under by all the hot sex. "I don't know if it's such a good idea." His playful and alluring smile oozed the words I'm going to fuck you good tonight. "Some people might not like that. Some people might get mad."

"I won't get mad." Daisy answered naively, the ringlets in her hair falling clumsily onto her shoulders as she balanced her tray in tact under her hand.

He knew she hadn't caught on yet. "No, what I mean is you know how a pendulum swings one way and for others it swings another way?" His hand made gestures from one side to the other moving his sexy body from right to left.

"Oh yeah!" She said believing she understood how having sex works. "We get all kinds of guys in here. Some with dicks that go this way and others that go that way." She trusted it was the curvature and the direction the cock was pointing. She was proud of how it was all coming to her.

"No, that's not what I meant either. What I mean is if one of these girls takes me back there and dances over me half naked..." He signaled with both of his hands towards Jagger. "My boyfriend here won't exactly be happy about it and I don't want to upset him."

Jagger raised one eyebrow up for a second by what came out of Sage's mouth. He quickly agreed and went along with the charade falling right into character. He leaned towards Sage while nodding up at the woman. "Yeah, I won't like that. Don't do it Sage."

"Oh!" she nodded obsessively with her thousand silver bracelets around her wrist shaking and clanking together in a beautiful orchestration. "I get it. Hey, you know I totally understand that. I love it! I'm from Texas and my cousin who lives there is gay. He's one of the greatest guys I know. He's one of my best friends."

Jagger's amused by her naivety.

"Yeah, so you can understand why it wouldn't be a good idea." Sage paused drawing up a polished smile, "But what we would like to do is this. Do you see those two girls down there chatting in the dark?" He pointed to Jacey and Becky in the distance who were watching the girls dancing and comparing notes. "The girl on the left with the darker hair, her name is Becky and she would love a dance. I'm going to give you some money here." He pulled bills out of his wallet. "You send her the best dancer you have."

"You got it!" Daisy's fervent spirit shouted out to the eons of energy around them as she worked her huge, red hooker pumps down towards Jacey and Becky.

Sage and Jagger burst out in silent open mouth laughter clasping their hands together in a harmonious hi-five. They reveled like two naughty sixteen-year-old boys who got away with vandalizing some property. Sage gripped and held onto Jagger's hand affectionately for seconds longer than what would've been conceived by some as crossing the line. He swiftly entered into an aura of silent infatuation for Jagger.

They looked on in the girl's direction with eager intent. They could see them in the dark at the other end of the club. Becky looked up at Daisy with concern. The boys watched Daisy's animated hands moving about the air as if she was explaining how to put together a model airplane. Becky let out a loud, colorful laugh and the boys could hear her shout in the distance. "Oh my god!" She brought both her hands to her mouth delirious.

Daisy placed her hand out to escort Becky to one of the back rooms where it's darker and more intimate. It's also where her stripper/dancer awaited. It's the place that only the seedy men go, the political judges, young college jocks, and psycho accountants who lock themselves up in their dark houses.

Jacey walked over to the bar to strike up a conversation with four of the stripper dancers. Some were waiting patiently for an available dance space on the podium in the center of the club, while others were on break. It was in the middle of the night and they weren't that slammed with patrons.

Sage moved out of the booth and gazed over at Jagger with a smile. "Come on babe." He put his hand out cupped towards Jagger insinuating he wanted to hold Jagger's hand. It was Sage's flirting opportunity to dance around what is dangerous to him. It's his way of being able to experience what's it's like to play intimate with another guy safely, and with one he trusts and can be close to more than any other. One he is completely comfortable with in opening himself up with in playful experimentation.

Jagger focused on Sage's hand before grabbing it as they showed each other off by roaming through the dark club to the bar area. They moved in closer next to each other as they walked. Sage took Jagger's hand and glided it up his arm to feel his bicep and their friendship enclosed them in a much more real way. Sage smiled wide getting an adrenaline rush. He is a real guy who is not afraid to be brave even if Jagger knows that it would never happen romantically for them. Jagger is pleased to have met a platonic friend regardless. They're role playing and being silly.

Some of the dancers looked over and beamed at the two hot dudes together at the bar. It was as if they've been a strong, close, power couple for years and the relationship only continues to get better.

It seemed as if hours had passed when Becky emerged out of the dark distance. She pulled up on her tight leather top, black leather mini skirt and black heels. "Oh my god that was so fucking good!" She fanned herself with her hand trying to bring her down from orgasm. "It was absolutely amazing!"

Jacey stood feet away from her laughing with her newfound Vegas stripper posse.

"I'm so wet below. I need a cigarette." Becky reached into her purse and pulled one out. "Her name was Candy and she said she could do things with me that she couldn't do with the guys. It was fucking amazing!" She took a drag of her cigarette. "She was basically dry fucking me."

Sage laughed and said, "I'm glad you liked it because Carla here..." He gestured to the smiling tall beauty that stood behind the clan. "She's going to take you to the back and give you another one."

"Oh my god!" Becky lost it being led away by Carla's hand, "I'm going to kill you guys." Becky and Carla disappeared into the dark for additional dry humping.

Later that night at around 5 am...

The foursome stumbled back to the two hotel rooms they had rented in one of the Vegas high rises. Jagger took the room that was vacant of the two while the girls and Sage went into the other one.

About ten minutes later, the boy couldn't wait because there was a knock at Jagger's door. It was Sage.

Jagger allowed the door to fall open and walked away from it. Sage followed in with gusto. "I'm staying here. Those girls are going to be chatty with each other and it will annoy me."

"Sure come on in, but there's only one bed." Jagger turned around to face him and motioned towards the huge King size bed pointing at him like a gun.

"That's okay we can sleep in the same bed." Sage was comfortable with his manhood, which pulled Jagger back in suspicion.

They could hear the girls giggling and talking loudly down the hall making their way into Jagger's room that was still open. Jacey said, "Hey guys. Let's go to the top of the hotel. There's a pool up there and we want to go swimming."

"It's five in the morning I'm going to sleep." Jagger climbed into the bed and under the covers. "You guys go ahead."

Sage looked at Jagger and at the girls, then leaped up and jumped onto the bed. "I'm staying here with Jagger."

Becky looked at Jacey dumbfounded for a split second wondering if Sage meant more. She was onto him. They didn't need to say anything, because Jagger read it on her face.

Becky thought it was strange that Sage wanted to stay with Jagger instead of with the girl he was dating, Jacey. "Fine, we'll see you tomorrow." She said as they both made their exit.

"It is tomorrow." Jagger mumbled.

"Nah, who cares about them?" Sage jumped up off the bed and walked over to the door latching it shut in everyway imaginable. He locked Jagger in the room like a wanted prisoner.

Sage walked back into the room and slipped off his jeans, revealing his muscular and toned legs. He walked into the bathroom leaving the door open. Jagger could hear the shower turn on while Sage talked about how much fun the strip club was.

The door of the bathroom wasn't facing Jagger, but he knew it was left open. He heard Sage climb into the shower and the sound of the water rushing out and running down Sage's hard naked body. *'Fuck. Why is he doing that? Why didn't he shut the door?'* Jagger tried to wipe the image out of his mind, but he wanted to get in there with him. *'Sage is fucking hot and it's a waste that he's into girls.'*

Sage stepped out of the shower, put a towel around his waist, and walked out into the room where Jagger was. He did that on purpose. He wanted Jagger to see. He's such an exhibitionist and getting a rush from it. There was nothing needed out in the room. All he did was come out to open a few of the empty drawers and fumble with the TV remote. He stood there with the towel around his waist switching the channels that only revealed how to play black jack and get around the Vegas strip.

Sage disappeared out of Jagger's view back into the bathroom and came out in his black silk boxers.

Oh fuck.

Oh yum.

Shit.

He took quick steps that moved into a run and jumped onto the bed. He stretched out on his side around Jagger.

"Hey." He said in a lowly, flirtatious voice crawling over the bed and climbing underneath the covers.

Jagger scratched his forehead and looked down trying not to look or he'll be too aroused. "O-Kayyy, yeah, hey."

Sage brought up a topic of discussion surrounding the whole same-sex attraction thing and how he's fine with it. He said that he has never done anything with a guy, but that he's supportive of it and likes Jagger. He said his two lines of support and never dwelled on it again.

He's amazing in Jagger's eyes, not because he's hot or because they're into each other, but because their personalities and interests are similar. They have the same amount of risk-taking, which is a lot. And they are both ready to leave the casino or the party at the same time. They are like super close brothers.

Sage reached over to switch off the light. Jagger tried his best not to stare at his naked skin, but everything about Sage was arousing to him. He absorbed the heat off his body like a sponge and wanted his body close to him all night. Jagger stripped down to his boxers while in the bed.

Sage got comfortable and adjusted to move closer towards Jagger as if he was making it happen by thinking it. Sage talked a little about what they should all do when they wake up. He simultaneously took another opportunity to move physically closer to Jagger.

Sage's arm brushed against Jagger's back and stayed there.

Jagger's eyes opened and his back was towards Sage who was nearly spooning him.

Oh, damn. Seriously?

Jagger jolted a little bit and tried to get comfortable. Sage moved around him to get even more comfortable. This was by moving his hand onto Jagger's side a little with affection. Jagger was thinking hard about other things so as not to grow an erection, but it was too late. He was growing.

Fuuuck, what is he doing?

Sage noticed that Jagger didn't jolt or shout with a '*hey now just what the hell do you think you're doing?*' He took that as a clue to move his arm around Jagger some more. It was the first time he ever showed physical affection with another male this drastically before. He was getting a real rush of adrenaline inside and wanted to test it out.

Minutes passed and they both grew quiet. Sage initiated another intimate action with Jagger. He wrapped his left leg around Jagger tight like a spider dragging his body up against his solid web. Jagger's full bubble ass was pressed against Sage's crotch area firm. Sage moaned trembling slightly enjoying the hotness of

Jagger's ass pressed against where his cock is. Sage stunned himself as he discovered he was growing hard.

"Fuck. You gotta be kidding." Sage whispered excited into the back of Jagger's neck chuckling nervously. The heat from his breath and voice warmed every cell of Jagger's. Sage couldn't believe how fucking hot Jagger felt.

Jagger felt Sage's bulge get fatter and begin to grow significantly. It was like a huge stabbing rock. Sage moved his body against Jagger's body slow, hard and strong. It was several smooth pulsating thrusts as he simulating fucking him. Sage's mind wandered reaching near faint over how hot this was making him feel. He expected it a bit, but not to the point of becoming lightheaded. Jagger sensed Sage's breath move behind his neck. Sage brushed his lips against it in a subtle way holding it there.

Sage continued to drive his body into him with his arms and leg wrapped around Jagger not letting go. His kisses behind Jagger's neck and upper back got hotter, longer and more passionate.

Jagger moved his body and head a little slightly towards Sage. Sage's lips took over Jagger's lips in a succulent kiss. Their tongues pushed their way into each other's mouths immediately and stayed in there longer over each kiss. Jagger's heart pounded with excitement to know what it was like to kiss Sage. Sage's mind blew up into an array of fireworks.

Sage's body found its way onto Jagger's and this time Jagger's legs wrapped around Sage's body while they continued to kiss and make out for awhile. Sage explored down Jagger's body with his hands.

Jagger moved his hands up and down the sides of Sage's body and around onto his back while Sage simulated fucking Jagger. They continued with their mouth exploration as they moved up and down on each other fucking without penetration. Jagger could feel Sage's heart pounding rapidly against his own chest and heard the vibrations of his moaning.

Jagger's hands found their way onto Sage's boxers. Sage's erect cock was wet seeping through his boxers and onto Jagger's skin. Jagger pulled Sage's boxers off slowly a little of the way down and glided his hands down over his bare ass. Sage loved how this felt and he moved his body upwards over him. Jagger continued to kiss him down his neck and all over his chest. Jagger could see Sage's smile wide in the dark.

Jagger pulled Sage's boxers clear down to feel his cock out in the open and against his skin. Sage moved his body upwards slowly feeling the sides of Jagger's body. He slid his cock into Jagger's mouth with amazing ease. His cock slid in and out of his mouth tight until his balls slapped against Jagger's face. Jagger tasted every good bit of him knowing this could be the last time.

He sucked him for nearly five minutes when Sage couldn't contain it anymore. He pulled his cock out of Jagger's mouth and ejaculated cum all over Jagger's chest. He moaned loudly, "Agh! Fuck yeah!" Sage leaned down kissing Jagger and then laughed. "Damn it guy. I'm sorry that happened quick."

Jagger rested his hand on Sage's shoulder above him, "Never apologize."

Sage reached down feeling Jagger's cock up. "Wow. This is what it feels like." He stroked it while kissing Jagger until he came as well.

Sage put his arm around Jagger. "That was the fucking best!" He paused. "I've never been sucked like that by a girl." He laughed.

Only a guy can please another guy because they know how they like it. The same way only a girl understands how she likes it. Sage jumped into the shower again, but this time pulled Jagger in with him. He headed back to the bed even more comfortable with each other.

"I'm not gay or anything." Sage proceeded to say, "And it would be fine if I was, but there's something about you that defies that. Maybe I'm bi. Eh who cares. I can't explain it. You're amazing. You're the only guy I've ever fantasized about and I couldn't contain myself. I thought if I'm going to experiment it would have to be with him. I didn't think I would nail you."

Jagger laughed, "You were planning this!?"

Sage moved his hands over Jagger's body and massaged his chest and stomach. He worked his way into his boxers, running his hand down to grab and feel Jagger's cock. He stroked it slowly trembling at the intensity of what a cock felt like. "You're fucking sexy. Your personality is not like anyone I've ever met. I don't know what it is, but it fucking turns me on. And I've never thought that about another guy ever! I have to keep saying that."

"You don't need to label it with anything." Jagger assured him. "That's for other's to wrestle with. This is what it is and nothing more. An experience. A connection with another soul."

Sage smiled liking that. He leaned into Jagger's lips. "Let me kiss you some more." Sage tested Jagger's lips and pushed his tongue sweetly into his mouth moaning at how good it felt.

Although that was the hottest moment for him, Sage and Jacey were at complete odds the rest of the trip arguing with one another. On the way home Sage had enough of Jacey's bitching and opted to sit in the back seat with Jagger. He leaned his head on Jagger's shoulder, closed his eyes, and went to sleep. He wasn't getting along with Jacey anymore as she was too high maintenance by starting little arguments over nothing. He was over her and now into Jagger. They arrived in L.A. to drop Sage off first. He pulled his bags out of the car and looked up at Jagger. "I'll call you alright?"

Everyone was quiet. Jagger felt awkward and looked down and away, then into Sage's eyes with a nod of assurance giving him the okay to call.

Sage and Jacey didn't speak after that day, but that was the beginning of Jagger and Sage's friendship.

Sage wasn't into guys on a physical level, but he was into sex and found Jagger to be damn good looking and erotic. He couldn't stop imagining what it would be like to kiss him and fuck that hot ass of his. He finally got the opportunity to explore it and the experimenting was just that. Their friendship grew tight spending every week together. At the end of the third year of their friendship, Sage announced he had a huge job offer back home in New York City. Jagger didn't like that everyone kept moving away from him. It made his soul grow harder. Sage made a pact to call him regularly and a few times a year they'd take turns visiting each other for a weekend or more. They kept that pact. Eventually Sage met the woman of his life. He made Jagger his Best Man at his wedding.

CHAPTER 5

Summer Loving

Flash Forward to the Present

Jagger sits up on a beach chair on his balcony under the hard beating sun with a good book. His surfboard stands up against the railing near him. It's got water and some sand on it as if he's just come back from the beach. His notepad sits on a nearby small table in case any good ideas come to mind. He has his shirt off and board shorts on. The energy is intoxicating around him. Swarms of beach crowds pull up on the street fighting over the little remaining parking spots available. He sits in the sun for so long that the little hairs on his arm begin to go from brown to blonde and sparkle when it hits the sun at the right angle. He sits up straight and tries to remain calm when he notices Garth coming around the bend.

Be cool. Don't let him get to you.

Garth moves towards him closer without a shirt on. His skin glistens with light beads of sweat under the sun. Jagger eyes the tattoo around his upper armband. It's a small Maori design. The Maori words or images symbolize a warrior, a place that Jagger is most at home with. He likes him even more.

Jagger doesn't want to stare at him for too long because he might be caught looking. He imagines gliding his tongue across Garth's tattoo, but then pulls back so he doesn't experience near faint while studying his body. The tones forming Garth's structure are in all the right places. The Coppertone boy one shade after white, but now the only part of his body that is his natural skin tone of white is his ass and frontal region. It's the rare section of his body that doesn't get to see any sun long enough to tan. He wants to yank his shorts off, throw Garth on the floor, and make love to him right there on the sidewalk.

He jots scribbling notes down in his pad. '*The guy who I think hates me is in love with me. I am love's fucking Hell. If a guy is into you and he's shy, he is probably more likely to approach you and start up a conversation if he's seen you around a lot.*'

A girl wearing a bikini top and biking shorts walks briskly with her headphones on while smiling at Garth. It screams sex.

Jagger watches Garth head down to the beach to his lifeguard tower. He closes his eyes in the sun visualizing his arms around him. His soul breathes in every inch of him while imagining the feeling of Garth's breath on his skin. He considers himself lucky that he gets to see him for a few seconds. That's a few seconds that turns his day that was once upside down into something completely right. He no longer inhabits his body. He soars above it. When Garth crosses his path he feels incredible strength. Garth's eyes make Jagger's soul tremble with love. Before he knew his name he had to find out what it was so he could at least know whose name to call out when he ejaculated.

When Jagger is in love with someone he doesn't want to have sex with them right away. He wants to be with them, get to know them and have the most amazing foreplay that leads to euphoric lovemaking at a later date.

This ends with some hard fucking. He offends some people by using rough language and talking about sex. What he especially wants is love. He wants to hold someone in the end. He knows not to give up on the idea of Garth. If it's out there enough, maybe it'll come true. Never give up and never throw the baby out with the bathwater.

Troy moves out onto the balcony breaking Jagger out of his trance. He sits up on the ledge. "So, Evan just sent me a text. You know that guy that I went out with the other day. It says, 'Hi, what are you up to?' What should I say?"

"Uhhh. What are you wearing?'" Jagger says.

Troy types it in and sends it. "I didn't tell you we had phone sex the other night."

Troy's phone beeps with a text. He looks down to read it. "Oh!" He laughs, "Now he goes, 'boxers, why?' How should I respond to that?"

"Boy he responded fast. That dude is horny."

"Perfect! That's what I'll say." He types it in.

Jagger rolls his eyes amused and directs his attention back to his book.

"Ooo! He says, 'You can have it. It's all yours.'" Troy jumps down off the balcony ledge. "You know what, I got to go." He runs off chuckling. Jagger knows where he is headed and laughs silently to himself.

Evan is twenty-three years old. He isn't exactly overweight, but he carries much of it in his belly. It isn't a typical beer gut. It looks like the guy is carrying a baby. Troy knows this isn't healthy and wants to help, because other than that slight distinction the guy is attractive to him in all other ways. Troy is a sucker for a guy who can talk a good game and Evan talks a good game. One night, Troy and Evan were lying in bed, talking all night, and then they fell asleep together. Troy tried to put his arm around the guy, but had to keep pulling away because he couldn't breathe being that close to him. When he kissed him this moved them into a sexual position. Evan climbed on top of Troy smashing his rib cage as he pounded his body. Troy attempted to adjust his body and breathe in-between his grinding, but it was no use. Luckily, less than a minute later, he felt something wet squirt on him. Evan had cum on him. It was a world record in under a few minutes. Troy barely got his clothes off when Evan let out a gasp and fell on top of him. Troy tried to push him up and off him so he could get some air. The next day Troy's rib cage felt bruised from the incident.

SEXY LIFEGUARD DUDE

Jagger lies in bed waking up to a shot of a nude babe magazine in his eye line. He looks on at the woman spread eagled in the magazine from a distance and his morning wood grows thick and stiffens. He fantasizes that her wet pussy drips down his cock while he thrusts in and out of her. Her hands move over his chest punching it while he fucks her. In real time, he pulls his thick growing cock from out of his Calvin bottoms and plays with it awhile stroking it to this image. This goes on for a few minutes when he stops and stands up. He knows that if you wait to ejaculate it'll be that more explosive when you finally do cum.

Jagger pulls his boxers back on, throws on some blue denims, a dark T-shirt, and heads outside. While outside, his face lifts upwards towards the light breeze which hits his aura from all angles. He meditates on the sky in contemplation. It is clear and stretched out into oblivion. The Sun is hot and beating down strong with force. He loves it when it's hot as he is hornier than usual. When it's cold, he wants to lay cuddled with you. When it's hot, he wants to strip down and fuck you.

He can be self-absorbed, but he pulls out his flaws on a daily basis while others praise him. They see something he's never seen, but he does attempt to see what good he has to offer. If he looks close enough he might catch that bit of goodness they see in him.

He walks over to his truck to pull some CD's out to play in his house. He sits in his truck with the door open watching the waves crashing in the distance hitting the white sands. The seagulls fly around circling a section down on the beach. He climbs back out of his truck and drags himself back towards his place slowly. Garth approaches him on the sidewalk. Jagger stares right at him directly into his eyes without shying away this time. He wasn't paying attention and hadn't noticed he was walking in his path. Jagger's eyes study Garth's arms and his muscles. His eyes move down over his body photographing it for the future. What would it be like to go for a ride for life with this gentle beauty? He watches Garth's eyes shift color with the brightness of the sun. Garth's hands rest comfortably in the pockets of his lifeguard shorts as he makes his way to work. Lifeguard station number sweet sixteen. Garth notices Jagger and buckles up. He's aware of how often they keep running into one another and goes for it. "Hello mate."

Talk. Jagger. Talk. Fuck.

Jagger's eyes grow bigger dilating in love. Garth's hello causes Jagger to smile. This lights up Garth's world even though Jagger is completely oblivious of the mutual effect he's having on him.

"What's up?" Jagger nods only able to say two words.

They both crisscross passing each other like two ships in the night. Garth heads down the path on his way to work the beach. Jagger makes his way back inside his house in shock that Garth spoke to him. Maybe it was only two words, but hey, he knows they are making progress.

Jagger doesn't realize the sexuality he conveys even when he's vulnerable and not just when he's combative. His highly perceptive and open personality wraps around others and they become drawn to his often attentive nature. He has a rare way of making people feel important. Guys sense the hot passion beneath the surface, and that's his playing card, the star quality sex appeal he has without knowing. It gives him that level of strength that radiates and explodes all over you like cum.

BIG ROMANTIC GESTURES

Four friends get together to shoot the breeze at the local Beached Hut hang out spot. Rock and roll music plays in the restaurant that turns into a beach bar by nightfall. They move through the packed place to a familiar spot.

"This guy called me, but he didn't leave a message." Jagger announces.

Troy chimes in, "If he doesn't leave a message he's trash."

"I got a sharp pain of depression right after it." Jagger admits.

Slade says, "I get that every time I have to call a date back."

Troy swigs his drink and faces the boys. "Not actually into the fetish thing, but I do collect sneakers. Oh! And they need to make sure that what they're "looking for" really IS what they're looking for. Edit: Just to clarify, if you're NOT in the 18-25, swimmers, athletic, muscular category and White-esque, Hispanic, then I'm probably not interested in anything physical."

"That's so limiting." Jaggers smiles.

Slade shrugs, "Me? I only enjoy sex. So how about friends? Fuckbuds. Fuck relationship. I don't know. I don't care. Call me and we'll take it from there."

"To the point. I like it. Easy pleasy." Jagger adds.

Russell says, "Boats, quads, guitars, beaches and lakes. If you're an Aero Hydraulic Technician even better. My type ain't here in this bar and the prisons aren't close enough."

Jagger slams back at them. "I need a dude with class, respect and dignity. Age is irrelevant. Maturity is."

Slade is cool and in complete command of himself. He cringes at the thought of anyone attempting to do anything romantic for him. He makes a mock vomit in the trash at the whole notion of romance. He remembers one guy who left a card in between some paintings he bought him. The card was an expression of his love for him. He couldn't figure out how the guy had pulled out love out of their fucking.

One of Russell's ex-boyfriend's used to drive an hour to leave a flower on the windshield of Russell's car early in the morning before he woke up. The fact that the guy got up so early in the morning to perform that tiny gesture spoke volumes to him.

Troy's closest thing to romance was a guy attempting to get into his pants. He would've preferred the guy did something drastic that showed him how into him he really was.

Slade recalls his most recent bout of love. A guy was sucking him off, then stood up, and waved his cock in Slade's face. He said, "Suck it." Slade was hoping the guy wouldn't ask because the cock looked nasty. He thought it's only fair he return the favor. So he held his breath and went for it for about ten-seconds hoping that would do it. "Okay there."

Slade explained that they didn't have sex because they were merely sucking each other off. Jagger disagreed and went home to write a column about it.

ORAL SEX IS NOT THE NEW SEX

There are those who believe that oral sex isn't actual sex. They believe because it's not intimate that it's also not cheating.

Fact: Oral sex is sex. Oral sex is intercourse. Oral sex is personal.

There are others, particularly young people as young as twelve and thirteen, who believe that oral sex isn't sex. Therefore, most of them are doing it and writing it off that it's okay because it's not sex.

One isn't more moral than the other.

There is a myth being spewed out there that is teaching young people that oral sex is not sex and that it's less moral. Parents and schools certainly aren't discussing it. They are having kids, but doing it irresponsibly. Is sex a matter of degrees?

They say he still has his virginity because he's only had oral sex. It makes no difference whether you're lying down or sitting up. The bottom-line is you've had sex.

If you're involved with someone and you have oral sex with someone else, then you have cheated. If it's not then why aren't you telling your lover you had oral sex with someone else if you don't feel it's cheating? It's still a sexual act.

CHAPTER 6

The Desert Fling

Brandon is thirty-three years old, amazingly cut with muscles rippling over his tight little body. He's shorter than average, ranging around five-foot-four. He is a walking symbol of hot sex, and a smile that lights up with three dimples. He's a charmer who got more than his fair share of things when he was little nearly getting away with murder because of his looks.

Slade took notice of him when he was staying in the desert one weekend. Brandon was initially afraid to make a move because Slade has that affect on people. When Brandon moves, he moves with a hip groove to his step. A thin, white, wire stretches across his upper naked torso and perfect frame. The wire plays the best def jams out of the mini player he has hidden somewhere in those hot shorts of his.

Out by the pool deck overlooking a view of the Desert Mountains that envelope the both of them like God's arms, Brandon moves past Slade. He has a slight and subtle smirk that features his beautiful big lips that widens a few centimeters as he smiles. Slade had kept his shorts on all day. It was nine at night in June and too hot to put the rest of his clothes on. The temperature in the air had cooled down to a warm eighty degrees. Slade slips into the Jacuzzi underneath the Full Moon light. The air is quiet and the sky is eminently dark and infinite. The stars are all visible without the distraction of the big city lights. Slade tilts his head back and zones out. There is no one else around and he is finally able to fully relax alone.

After a few minutes, he hears movement entering into the water. He sleepily draws his eyes open to the beauty before him. Brandon is approaching him in the water and takes a seat right next to him. Slade adjusts his body and moves a few inches away. This doesn't stop Brandon who smiles at him. Under the water, Brandon pulls his own shorts off, although with the bubbles it is impossible to see anything. Brandon stands up and puts his shorts on the landing area outside the Jacuzzi. The water reaches up to his waist and Slade glances at his tan line. Brandon uses that opportunity to flex because that's what boys do when they like you. They show off their feathers like a male peacock. Slade appears solid on the outside and excited with butterfly nerves on the inside. Brandon leans into his ear. "You're a sexy fox and I'm going to get you."

"Oh yeah?" Slade says, "You're confident with yourself there, aren't ya. We'll see."

"Yeah, we will definitely see. You're fucking hot." Brandon stands back up in front of Slade. Slade reaches his hand over to Brandon's leg and feels up the side of it. There is too much lust burying him in a ring of fire. He moves his hand behind Brandon urging him to move closer to him. Brandon stands between Slade's legs and leans down to kiss him. They fall into the water making out as the heat races through their body. Lust is a difficult thing to turn away from for Slade. We are animals unable to see beyond nothingness at times, but that's two minutes you're taken to another place called Paradise.

HEIKE'S PROVERBS

The boys love hanging out at Russell's house. It's big and private. It has a pool and a Jacuzzi in the backyard. Jagger lays out on a beach chair alone. He barely hears the echo of a tire screech into the driveway.

Troy pushes open the back gate to the pool area. He immediately strips down to his boxers exposing his lean young body. Charging forward and curling up into a ball in the air he effortlessly lands in the pool. The explosion of the water splashes everywhere hitting Jagger.

"Hey! You fuck!" Jagger shouts. "I'm sitting here."

Troy's head pops out of the water giggling like a child. "You're already wet you may as well jump in."

"I wanted to enjoy this gorgeous sun."

"Come on!" Troy splashes him more.

"Bitch ass." Jagger hops up and walks around the pool. "You are fucked." He sits at the edge of the pool dipping his feet in. He moves slowly into the pool and drowns his whole body underneath the surface of the water. He comes up for air and is face to face with Troy's smiling wonder.

Later that night at the Beached Hut, four friends get together to absorb their familial love. Heike, the wacky German cocktail waitress that loves the group waltzes over to the four boys talking over each other and says, "We should all have grenade launchers mounted to the roof of every car. There's population control for ya!" She places all of their drinks next to each one of them. "And someone please tell me why these dumbasses and old people stop on the damn entrance ramp onto the freeway? If you drive a dozen miles under the posted speed limit, you should be charged with reckless driving. It is dangerous!" Her mouth opens wide letting out a loud animated laugh. Slade smiles. Russell laughs. Jagger and Troy stare at her blankly.

Slade is finding himself more promiscuous if that's even possible. "Travis, that new guy I met the other night at the bar loved sucking my cock. He told me how he could keep it in his mouth forever. The only problem was he couldn't do it right. He kept scraping my dick with his teeth. I wanted to pull my cock out and jack off myself."

He did have a point. Sometimes sex is so bad that you're better off doing it alone.

Troy looks down at the palm of his hand and mumbles. "I need to get fucked."

Troy's two-month drought had caught up with him. He is ready to lie in the middle of the bar and let someone do it to him in front of everybody. Sometimes when it's been so long since you've last had it, you're ready to do it with anybody who will touch you no matter how bad they are at it. This is why some resort to hooking up when they haven't had a relationship for quite some time. They need to be touched, as it's been too long. We all have needs including love and affection. For some, this is more than others.

Russell takes a drink. "What happened to that guy you were with?"

"That's not happening." Troy explains, "He likes me, but I don't know if I'm interested is all. We've kissed once though."

Slade boasts. "I sometimes forget to lock the door and a guy sneaks in and can see me stroking my cock in a reflection in the hallway mirror. He takes off his clothes and begins playing with himself. He gets that cock nice and hard while moving closer to the bedroom where he can see me naked."

The boys stare at Slade expressionless and bored as if he were discussing quantum physics.

Troy would rather be naked in public since it's not his style to have a meaningless hook up.

It's not meaningless to Slade who adjusts his balls making fun of the man's voice. "The guy goes, *'there were other intense aspects, but that hugging was full of emotion I don't know what was going on, but I felt we each expressed something heartfelt in the hugs.'* I wanted to vomit. I said to him, get over yourself dude there was nothing there. We just fucked!"

Jagger nods agreeing with him. "That's the worst. When someone you hook up with tries to attach themselves to you. It's like a stray cat you feed once. They're suddenly at your door every goddamn day. They want to see you 24/7. It's embarrassing for them. Why reduce yourself to the level of a fool?"

Heike places some appetizer finger foods onto the table. "Why do we have to make speeding tickets profitable for the police? Don't they get enough allowance? I'd say more than the budget of education and welfare. Why don't we give them all a donut when they stop someone going ten miles over the speed limit? Maybe then they'll start to look for murderers and stuff instead! Ah-ha-ha-ha!"

Jagger is cold and vacant. "Or how about anyone that holds their cell phone to their ear while driving. They should be pulled over and not given a ticket, but it should be treated as if it were a DUI?"

Heike's smile goes down at the ominous tone. "Oh okay. I must think about that one."

CHAPTER 7

Caden: The Malibu Cobra

Caden is twenty-six and a Pro Surfer in Malibu. This is where the hardcore surfers tend to venture to in the L.A. area. Caden has the typical bleached blonde hair thing going with the beach tanned skin. The bangs that fall over his face, hazel eyes and cut up abs. Caden loves getting a rise out of Jagger because that's when he knows he is finally getting the attention he craves from him. Jagger is not someone who strokes your ego and rarely hands out compliments so when he actually does give one, then everyone listens. Caden is always bringing up his abs trying to electrify Jagger with them. Jagger has to say, "That doesn't impress me. It's your grey matter I like."

When they are together, they get along splendidly. When they aren't together, Caden goes crazy. He needs Jagger with him around the clock, which is impossible. Jagger likes him though and wants to explore the connection with him a little.

It was about two weeks into knowing Jagger when Caden received his first taste of what he was up against.

Jagger doesn't click over in the middle of a call unless it's a call he's expecting. He finds it rude to veer attention off the call he's already on unless necessary. Jagger was on the phone with Russell. Meanwhile beeps are continuously happening throughout their call to signify that other calls are coming in and falling into voice mail.

Jagger and Russell hang up at about 10:30 that night and like any business Jagger starts retrieving his other messages.

Jagger mumbles excited, "Yes! Caden called." He proceeds to call him back.

"Hey!" Jagger shouts.

"Oh, hey." Caden replies with a cold and ominous tone. Something is clearly bothering him.

"What's up?" Jagger says smiling, but getting nothing but dead air on the line. He can hear Caden breathing then a stressed out exhale. *Yeah, blow it out my brother.* "What's wrong? Why are you agitated?"

Caden finally works it up, "You know, I called you at 6:30." His tone is nasty and ready to pick a fight. Jagger is thrown off. *What in the fuck?*

"No, it was 8:30!" Jagger slams.

"No, it was 6:30!" Caden says thrashing back in an attempt to one up him.

"No buddy it was 8:30! My phone tells me what time the call came in." Jagger smacks back.

Caden is quiet not knowing how to top it. "Whatever. Where were you this whole time?" He asks in a condescending and ugly tone that screams Ike Turner.

"I was on the fucking phone!" Jagger throws him a left, because they are both getting good at this.

"This whole time!" Caden hits back.

"Yes, this whole time!"

It's completely silent except for Caden's repetitive exhale stress stuff. Jagger's voice grows cool. "Now you have me on the phone, so go ahead and talk."

Caden doesn't know what to say as he thought he had the upper hand. "Actually, I have to return some of these other calls I'll call you next week."

"Don't bother." Jagger hangs up the phone and then throws it across the room in an annoyed rage.

He paces like an angry Tiger, then picks up the phone off the floor and starts to dial. "Hey, Slade? You are not going to believe this shit."

The next day when Jagger awoke around 9am, he found seven text messages from Caden apologizing. Jagger quickly labeled him the new text message King. Caden sent him things like he didn't know what came over him and he guesses he really likes Jagger and stuff.

Jagger mumbles to himself. "No, not okay. Not okay to act like that."

Caden doesn't have that many bad qualities, but he is possessive in a scary way. Jagger typically doesn't mind a little possession and in fact bathes in that intensity from a lover he has the hots for. When it reaches a point where you're insulting him, then you're running into a heap load of trouble. It'll fly at you from all angles if you mess with it.

Jagger later said to Slade, "It's not like I'm out parading around, fucking around, and being bad. I'm busy working. The possessiveness thing is totally baseless."

He waited a whole day before he called Caden back. Then he went for it and called him. "Hello Caden." Jagger said in a tone that let Caden know he's in trouble.

"Hey." Caden said trembling a little, "I didn't think I was going to hear from you again, and I wanted to."

"Yeah, well we need to talk, but I can't get into it right now. I'm on my way to a wedding. The irony. I'll call you afterwards. There's something that needs to be addressed here." Jagger was all business.

"Okay, can you tell me now?" Caden pleads.

"No. There's no time and I need time to get into it. I don't want to have to stop in the middle."

"You're scaring me."

"Don't be scared." Jagger says. "I'll call you around 7p."

"So at 7p then?" Caden implies on the dot not realizing his anal retentiveness.

"Yes, around 7p okay." Jagger corrects him.

A couple of hours pass and Jagger calls Caden up who is extraordinarily way too chipper for his cool surfer vibe. He knows he is in for it and doesn't want to blow it.

Jagger lets into him trailing off one rant after another, "....and who the fuck do you think you are...."

Caden interjects, "I would think that you would be flattered that someone likes you that intensely."

"Flattered? No, alarmed!"

Caden apologizes profusely explaining that he can't help it. When he likes a guy, he can be very forceful. He admits that he shouldn't have behaved like that. Jagger decides to let him in and deem it out some more. He is drawn to him, but hesitant after the strange phone call the night before. The two continue on with dating each other anyway.

The next day, Jagger heads over to Caden's place only to discover that he forgot the code to get past the front gate. He can see some people sitting by the pool in the near distance. They know he is trying to get in, but are too lazy to get up and open the door.

"Excuse me!" Jagger shouts. "Is it at all possible that any of you shits could be polite enough to let me in?"

A goofy lady with a dog and blackjack cards falling out of her purse gets up. She walks over with a smile that looks as if it's been there for so long that she doesn't even realize that it's there anymore. It's frozen on her face until all eternity. She holds the door open for Jagger.

"Fuck." He utters under his breath and then changes his tone to politeness, "Thanks." He locks eyes with the goofy lady. She senses something deeper in him that is masked by the bad boyish presence. She tilts her head towards him with that pasted smile. He walks up the stairs stampeding into the already opened door to Caden's place.

Caden stands with a cocky smirk, shorts and no shirt against one of the kitchen drawers. He moves toward Jagger who is dumping his crap on the floor pacing and mumbling fuck under his breath every so often as if he has Tourette syndrome.

"Baby," Caden says with a tender smile. He approaches Jagger and takes his face into his hands sweetly, "Baby," his lips kiss Jagger's repeatedly. "What did you say out there?"

"Well, they were just fucking sitting there. They couldn't see I was trying to get in?"

Caden shakes his head smiling and continues to kiss him. "I have to live here. You just can't do that." He soothes Jagger's short temper.

"I know," Jagger replies agitated, but with a softer voice. "I'm sorry, but you didn't see it." He explains, "I've been fucking stressed all day and all week."

"Come here." Caden says softly putting his arm around Jagger leading him to a chair, "Come sit here."

Jagger sits down and studies Caden. "What? Why?"

"Shhhh." Caden says with an enticing smile. He kneels down and begins to unbutton Jagger's jeans slowly.

"Whoa, what're you doing?" Jagger grabs Caden's hands to stop him. Caden pushes them away because he is getting in there whether Jagger likes it or not. Jagger attempts to stop him, "I don't know. Isn't this too soon?" He can't believe he wants to wait it out. Caden is honestly a babe and how could one refuse when a hot guy insists on getting into your pants? And that guy is your boyfriend.

"Shhh, don't worry about it, just relax and let me take care of you for a change." The thought of being taken care of is attractive to Jagger. He learned to set up for himself from an early age due to parental neglect. He had never had someone wanting to take care of him before. This was another reason he is drawn to Caden.

Jagger's thick cock pops out of his jeans for Caden to see who takes the next cue and slides it into his mouth. Caden sucks on it for twenty minutes, sliding Jagger's thick cock in and out of his mouth while fondling his balls. Caden is very patient as he makes love to his cock up and down. Jagger leans back in the chair and debates whether to have him stop or keep on trucking. He drifts off and lets it happen until he shoots his cum all over his own torso.

Caden is falling head over heels for Jagger who is moving at his own steady slow pace. Jagger isn't seeing anyone else, but Caden feels he might as well be since he never gets to see Jagger as much as he likes. When they are together they have fireworks and perfect bliss. When they aren't together Caden continues to have fits of rage. He is tired of not being able to talk to or see Jagger who is oblivious to the growing frustration his dating companion is harboring.

Not long afterwards in another incident and on another day, Jagger checks his messages while at home and notices Caden had called. His face lights up again while he listens on, "Hey, it's Caden." His voice turns cold and nasty, "What a surprise. Voice mail again," he scoffs with annoyance. "Whatever." There is an abrupt click signifying he hung up the phone.

Jagger's face grows cold. "Why would you say that?" He shakes his head and his blood begins to boil. "That's it. Fuck this. I'm over this crap." He can't understand why Caden would continue to sabotage something that he feels is headed in a great direction.

Caden's phone rings and his voice mail plays. '*Fuck, of course it'll be his voice mail because he's pissed. He knows it's me calling. Damn it. More games.*'

"Um, yeah hi Caden, it's Jagger. I was hoping to get you on the phone or even stand face to face with you for this, but naturally you're not picking up. I'm sorry, but this is not working out. I like you, but I can't do this anymore. You obviously need someone 24/7 and I'm not that guy. You have a 50-item list of criteria on what you want in someone. I'm not that guy either. I think we know that this is it. Let's not keep going around in circles. I wanted to be dignified here and get you on the phone, but oh well, good bye. Thanks for everything."

The next morning Jagger drives off in his truck and lets his cell phone messages play. What a surprise Caden left one. It begins with a long pause, but Jagger could hear him breathing. Caden starts up with his low maintained voice, "I don't think I said I was looking for someone 24/7, but part of getting to know someone is spending time with them and at least talking to them and...," he breathes a heavy relentless sigh, ".....and going for two days without having heard from the person is wrong. I don't think it's an outlandish request for me to ask to talk to you at least once a day if even for ten minutes..."

Jagger shoots back in his car. "Yes it is. Yes it is!"

Caden's voice mail continues to play over Jagger's rant, "....all I'm asking is for you to give us a chance, because I want to do this with you Jagger you know I do." He says with intention, "I hope you'll call me back."

Jagger takes a deep breath mingled with irritation and feeling lured back in all over in repetition. He is moved by the invitation, but not knowing what to do. He calls Slade for his words of cryptic advice.

"Don't call him back." Slade advises, "It's going to happen again with the guy. You'll go back, then he'll be nasty and then you'll break it off. This has been going on for two months now. It's the same scenario."

"I know, but I do like him and we're fine when were together. He keeps pressuring me to commit and be with him every day, which I would love to, but I can't right now. I'm too busy."

"You guys will have to meet half way or forget it." Slade offers. "He wants you now. You want to move slowly and aren't even sure if you want him completely. Just fuck each other and enjoy yourself, but I say don't call him back."

"You know me though. I need closure." Jagger will at times be on the phone about to say goodbye to a caller, but then the cell phone drops the call a minute before they hang up. He has to call them back prompting whichever friend is on the line to laugh and say, "I know you need closure."

Jagger calls him back, "Hey, Caden."

"Heyyy." Caden is joyful with glee that his boy is calling him back.

"Look, we need to talk okay." Jagger tells him.

"What is it?"

"I like you, but I can't be pushed anymore like this. You need instant relationship and I don't know. Let's be friends for awhile and see how it goes. I have too much shit going on and I can't drag you into that. It will be awhile before I come around in the way that you want."

"Wow. Well I'm glad you're telling me this, because I was asked to go out on a blind date and was planning to cancel it, but now that you're telling me this I may just...."

"Oh hey, yeah go on the date." Jagger interrupts.

"I will now. I'm going to call the guy and say I will do it. Thank you. Thank you Jagger for telling me this, because I wasn't sure if I should or not and you've confirmed it."

"Oh, you're welcome!" They both sound abnormally polite and malicious in a subtle way. Jagger adds, "...and hey I hope this is the one and you guys have a romance that lasts a lifetime."

"Oh me too, I'm looking forward to it." Caden replies slyly with joy. "So, I'm going to call him and let him know were on and I'll call you back."

"Sounds good." Jagger says psychotically cheerful. "This will be great for you, because although I like you, there is no way I can do this thing right away. And you meeting this guy will be a good thing cause let's say that....."

Caden interrupts, "Wait. What did you say?"

"About what? Which part?"

"You were saying how you like me and..."

"Oh! Wait. No, I just mean that..." Jagger wriggles around.

"I'm canceling the date," Caden slams in, "Let me call to cancel and call you back."

"No, Caden you're misinterpreting."

"Whoa, whoa, whoa baby. Don't worry about it. You like me."

"Of course I do, but all I'm saying is...."

"I'm canceling the date." Caden explains, "You don't worry about that and I want you to come over. I'm going to cook dinner for you. What do you like?"

"Ah, Fuck. Look, see this is too fast. I think you should go on the date."

"Baby the date is gone. I'm canceling. Come over. Let me cook for you. We'll move at a slow pace its okay."

Jagger takes a deep breath feeling attracted to his sexy persistence and in wanting to cook for him on top of that. He loves romantic gestures and that scores big points in his world. "Ugh. Alright, alright, fine."

Caden works the kitchen with ease cooking for his Jagger. He is happy like a kid in a candy store.

Jagger gets up wanting to help and heads into the kitchen, "Hey, anything I can do?"

Caden smiles and moves over to Jagger and kisses him. "No, baby you just relax. I have it. I'm taking care of you." He grabs and holds Jagger's hand leading him to the living room to sit back and relax.

Jagger feels uncomfortable letting someone else take the upper hand. "You know I'm a little uneasy about this." He shouts from the living room.

"I can't hear you." Caden sings happily.

Jagger has never been used to anyone taking care of him. It's been that way since he was eight. Parents never home. Sometimes they'd work late into the evening or not come home at all. Occasionally, he would fix his own dinner. Here is a guy who wants to take complete care of him and it makes him uneasy. He likes it, but not sure what to do with it or how to respond to it.

Caden caters to him hand and foot, lighting candles, bringing everything to him and creating a magnificent feast. Hours after the romantic dinner, the two make out and then make love for hours in the bedroom. It's not sex, it is slow, passionate love making.

Jagger and Caden continue to grow more hot and heavy as the weeks pass. Caden is being very patient, but Jagger knows that the patience will eventually run thin again. He knows that Caden will only be able to agree with it for so long before he blows a gasket. He knows Caden is slightly faking it knowing he could be rewarded with Jagger forever, because he wants the prize now.

One evening while Jagger and Caden roll around on the floor laying on each other for hours talking, Jagger looks at the clock seeing it is 11:00 at night. He excuses himself as he has to get going soon.

Caden suggests, "Well, maybe one of these days you'll spend the night."

Jagger contemplates, "Yeah, I will. We will do that very soon."

One of Jagger's rules is never spend the night with a guy or let him spend the night with you unless you were seriously involved. It leads to complications, but Jagger is finding that the complications are already brewing.

They lay on the floor together when Jagger announces he's got to go. Caden pulls his arms and hands away from Jagger and brings them to his own body in a defensive move. He conjures up his passive aggressive hurt over the fact that Jagger has a life and obligations and has to leave. He's not okay with that. He wants him joined to his hip permanently.

Jagger finally gets up, "Okay, I better head out."

Caden stands up, "Yeah I understand. You got to go, you got to go. We'll take little, tiny itty-bitty, baby steps."

Jagger's eyebrows arch while leaning down to grab his shoes. He starts to put them on when Caden walks by and shoves him hard. Jagger loses his balance falling over a little onto the floor, but blocking it with one hand.

What the fuck?

Jagger shakes it off, gets back up and continues putting his other shoe on. He stands up and with exuberant strength charges at Caden. Jagger slams him against the wall. He uses the force of his forearm pressed against Caden's chest preventing him from moving. Then he does something that throws Caden off. He lifts Caden's shirt and kisses his stomach and up his chest. He rises up sucking on his neck, kissing his face and then his lips. Caden feels faintish and his arms fly to his side losing himself to Jagger. After minutes of kissing him all over Jagger moves up to Caden's ear and says with an angry quiet tone. "Don't push me."

Caden begins his infamous text messaging to Jagger, because on the third month of their dating this was easier for him to keep it going by hiding behind technology.

Caden texts: "Do you want to see the new Texas Chainsaw Massacre movie?"

Jagger wasn't up for a horror film, but wanted to see him regardless. He texts him back: "No, maybe something else."

"Yeah, whatever take care." Caden texts Jagger.

"*What? Oh for fuck sake. Here we go again.*" Jagger is short-circuited by Caden's attitude and officially tired of it. He texts back. "Oh because I won't see the movie you want to see?"

Caden texts: "Only you know what the problem is and only you can fix it. You should get some help. We're both good looking guys and you know we can get anyone."

"What are you talking about now?" Jagger texts done with this.

"Maybe you might want to move out of the bedroom with the next guy?" Caden hits him back.

"Oh I must've had it backwards. I thought it was my cock up your ass that you liked. This is a relationship by text message that I can't do. Get lost guy." Jagger texts.

"Thank you." Caden gives his final text response.

And that was that. No more Caden. The relationship that ended by text message. Jagger knew it would never work out from day one, but chose to ignore those thoughts and red flags. This isn't to say that Jagger is a saint as he could've put in a little more effort to meet half way. However, even though both parties need to compromise, Caden was a little too possessive too soon for Jagger's tastes. He added it up to be a matter of bad timing.

Caden spent the next few months publicly trashing Jagger. Jagger on the other hand paid no mind. He figured he must've been hurt deeply by this, but the flogging him had to stop. It had been months and Caden was still trashing him. If Caden used communication and called him to tell him how unhappy he was they might've been able to be adult about it and remain friends. Caden's attitude is if you don't sync up with me the way I want, then you can't sync up with anybody.

If it were possible, Jagger would've ran over his surfboard with his car, but the odds of it breaking were slim. It could be split in two if flown fifteen feet in the air and trampled on by the force of a wave, but not a car. He got a hold of Caden's surfboard and attempted to break it, but the most damage he was able to do was ding it. He thought about ways to have it slice through the surf while inflicting it, but it was no use. The statement was made and Caden's public attacks stopped after that. It was more out of fear of what else Jagger would be capable of if he didn't stop.

CHAPTER 8

Fantasy Turns to Madness

There are many out there on the hunt for love. They are serial daters, serial fuckers and have endless lists of requirements in a mate. Those people generally remain single for a long time. Jagger did not want to become one of those people and did not want to be a statistic. Sometimes it's better to throw the list away and have an open mind and open heart to the new experience that your date is offering, because no one will ever be as perfect as you.

The one that you didn't consider liking at first is the one who is more likely to be a match for you. You don't see that until about the fifth or sixth date. This is when the façade and the front you put on begins to strip away revealing the real you. Unfortunately, many people today give up immediately after the first or second date. You judge harshly and want instant gratification.

I'll call you means *I want to avoid you.* Guy's can be extremely romantic when they meet someone they like. They suddenly become unable to see beyond the beauty, which gets them into trouble. They see that the object of their desire is hot, sweet and loves to rock climb too, but that's where it stops. No other characteristics are allowed in. They come to realize it when they've invested too much time in the situation that they were all wrong for each other to begin with.

Jagger has the opportunity to have sex with most anyone, but lately he's been bored with it and is keeping an eye out for a quality dude. Who could qualify? He doesn't have a list of what he wants except that they be loyal, but no one he attracts in seems to fit the bill in having that one required trait. They all end up disappointing him by vanishing without a trace or revealing some unmanageable neurosis. He can't figure out if it's him or them.

They all want to reach over and touch his cock and he lets them because he wants to be touched. He wants love under his smoldering hard exterior. He knows that it's not love he's feeling with them. He is feeling something, so he lets them touch it.

When you're looking for a love mate, you tend to look for someone who is attractive first. It's a chemical reaction and your brain is suddenly triggered when you see them. Over time, the attraction factor becomes less important and other things about them become more significant such as communication style and similar interests and values. This might explain why connections formed suffer unable to last longer than a few weeks. You find each other extremely attractive and think you're in love. The reality sets in and you discover they are as flawed as everyone else in the world. You have an Americanized, fantasized, fairy tale view of what a romantic interest is supposed to be and therefore you are constantly let down, because it doesn't exist. You're looking for the next best thing, but instead you end up bouncing from person to person thus isolating yourself, your own life, and the people that have been around you.

Jagger was bummed out and worn by what happened with Caden. He knew that as long as he has his work out exercise routine, then he doesn't have to feel like a total piece of crap. He gears up to take a light jog on the sand. Heading out and moving into the zone with his music, he releases all that pent up aggression out into his physical routine.

Watching the waves crash as he jogs through the sand, he sees Garth hanging out of his lifeguard tower alone. Garth stands with his hands in his pockets at attention. Garth studies Jagger jogging towards him while life's soundtrack blares up in the background. Jagger can't look anymore or he'll trip and fall face forward into the sand. His fantasy is turning into madness. He focuses on slowing down his breath while Garth watches him not breaking away eye contact.

Jagger is suddenly distracted as he catches a woman wearing a tube top looking like some kind of tramp from Brooklyn smacking her gum in her mouth. She pulls up on her top that rests on her bouncing breasts without a strap. She has on blue jeans that go down to about her knee. Her huge heels make a loud noise every time they hit the ground to let others know she's there. Her other hand drags her nine year old daughter who wears a similar outfit.

Jagger reaches the foot of the boardwalk and moves to a stroll. He hopes to get inspired to write or come up with an idea for his next column. While there, he notices Garth standing out on his lifeguard tower from afar. Garth's eye contact lingers a little too long. Jagger sees Garth smile slightly embarrassed, then look elsewhere. Garth heads into his lifeguard tower, and comes back out with his surfboard. Out in the ocean, Garth climbs up on the surfboard and rides a wave showing off knowing that Jagger is watching. Jagger smiles a little studying him.

CHAPTER 9

Skater Boy

Trezner's long running crush on Jagger prompts him to finally ask him out. Jagger is always running into the 22 year old and they assumed a natural friendship. He will catch Trezner gliding on his skateboard, following him around, or racing to the beach with his surfboard. Jagger is reluctant to going on a date with him due to his age, but he knows it would make Trezner's day. It's not like he is going to marry him. However, he did wonder how they were going to get to the date. Would it be by skateboard? Still, he is love starved and needs some honest physical touch with someone who wants that from him with every cell of their body. There's no bigger drag than sleeping with someone who is just not that into you. Jagger needs you to fall into a bundle of nerves when you're about to sleep with him. This gets him off being adored like that. He accepts Trezner's proposition to go on a date.

They arrive at the Beached Hut in Hermosa Beach and move up to the bar together. Jagger asks the bartender for a beer. Trezner says he wants a real drink.

"Oh, then I'll have a real drink too." Jagger says to the bartender, "I need to be on his level. Give me a mixed Stoli."

They grab a seat and Trezner makes his first big dating faux pas. He tells Jagger all about his past bad relationship experiences. He divulges how he has a drinking problem and he drinks every chance he gets. "I'm being good in your company." Soon Trezner pulls out a cigarette, "Do you mind if I smoke? I don't smoke, but sometimes I like to have one when I have a drink."

"I don't care for cigarettes," Jagger explains, "but if it gets you through this. I also don't typically drink all that much either. I used to smoke occasionally when I was going through my rebellious delinquent phase."

Trezner can't understand why one has to go through the same bullshit routine when he meets someone he's attracted to. They're coy, shy and flirtatious. They make love once and are reduced to simply fucking and getting each other off every time after that. The romance dries up as quickly as paint dries.

Jagger tells him the trick is to keep the romance alive by putting in actual effort. This brings a smile to Trezner's face.

Trezner's ex boyfriend told him he would have to stop drinking or he'll ruin their relationship. The ex got tired of him calling him up late at night routinely wasted to the point where he couldn't understand what he was saying. Trezner wanted to be committed completely to him, but the guy kept implying that he himself wasn't ready.

Jagger said, "The guy is 38 and he's not ready? He may never be ready or he doesn't think that you're right for him."

"That's how I felt sometimes, like there was something wrong with me. That's why he never wanted to commit."

"No, there's nothing wrong with you. You were with the wrong guy that's all."

Trezner's eyes widen and he leans forward listening intently hoping he can absorb some of Jagger's insight to make him feel better.

"If a guy knows you're right for him he will go for it." Jagger recites to him, "There is no growing into it. You either are or you aren't."

Occasionally, Trezner escapes to use his cell phone in private to call or text his friends back. When he comes back he explains it wasn't an ex, just a friend of his. Jagger is too buzzed on the rough alcohol to allow it to get to him. He's silently aware that it's inappropriate though.

Trezner asks Jagger to join him and his friends to go to a hot new nightclub that opened up in the Hermosa Beach area.

Jagger wants to ditch him as too many dating mistakes were already made. He likes him as a friend, but that's it. He's not up for meeting his friends on a first date at some nightclub where everyone is getting sloshed and trying to fuck each other. That's one area where the differences in maturity are apparent. It's not an age thing. He's run into this problem with those older than him too.

Jagger is concerned that Trezner has had a few too many drinks. He knows Trezner's ability to roam about is already impaired, and to get to a club to drink even more is unacceptable. He politely ends the date, but not without offering to walk him home first.

Trezner is hurt and pulls away detaching himself from Jagger as they both exit the Beached Hut and onto the sidewalk.

"I'll see you later." Jagger says noticing that Trezner is bummed out as if he wanted more.

"Okay, yeah." Trezner approaches Jagger and falls into a hug with him. Jagger is confused and wraps his arms around him too. Trezner's growing boner presses against Jagger. Trezner backs away flushed with embarrassment realizing it's too late.

Jagger watches him falter walking away and can't stand it anymore. "Hey, Trezner"

Defeated and somber he utters sadly. "Yeah?"

Jagger's heart is stabbed by the sight of him. "Oh man, come here. Jesus."

Trezner drags himself back over to Jagger slouching and fragile, but being anchored by Jagger's self-assurance.

Jagger smirks and puts his hand on Trezner's shoulder. "Is something wrong?"

Trezner looks away, anywhere but Jagger's bracing eyes. "No, I'm fine." He takes a deep breath. "I guess I hoped for a little more with you is all."

Jagger nods a little removing his hand off Trezner's shoulder and goes in for it. He wraps his strong arms and aura around Trezner and moves in for a long kiss. The stars all fall and circle around them. Trezner's hard on pokes Jagger who wonders if the guy has on any underwear.

"That's it. Come on." Jagger tells him.

Trezner smiles, "Where are we going?"

"You're coming with me." Jagger's smile widens when he moves into his face. "I'm going to love you tonight."

Trezner lights up ecstatic and unable to believe it's happening.

Back at Jagger's place, the two engage in some erotic fantasy talk that doesn't stop....

Trezner wanders around the living room and makes a confession. "When I woke up this morning I was feeling good because I knew I was going to see you, but it would've been even better waking up next to you." Realizing what he said, "Sorry, I woke up a bit horny this morning I guess."

"If you only knew how horny I am in the mornings." Jagger says. "The hottest time to get me is in the middle of the night or in the morning. The steam is literally seething off my body. Growing up I used to wonder why it was more so during that time of the day than any other. Your body produces and builds up testosterone while you're asleep. You're less stressed and more relaxed. This is why there is a fantasy that some guys have about being woken up with their cock in your mouth. It's like Hello. I'm much cuddlier then too!"

"Whoa! Steam seething off your body?" Trezner says ready to fall over, "I guess I'll be spending the night. The thought of that makes me hard. I could tell when I first saw you that you would get wild and that thought turned me on beyond words."

Jagger sits down on one of the comfortable sofa chairs. Trezner walks over leaning over to kiss him. Jagger grabs his hand and pulls him on his lap. His hands glide over Trezner's body making him tremble. Trezner feels Jagger's cock growing huge against him.

Jagger loves physically absorbing someone, grabbing them and exploring every inch of their body. He loves getting rough as constant physical touch is like air to him. If he doesn't have it in a relationship or with someone, then he's as good as dead. Every part of him screams out for it every single day.

Trezner curls up against him. "You have me all worked up. When I'm not with you I will be jacking off to the thought of you. I hope that doesn't bother you."

"That doesn't bother me. I may be called studious or difficult, but some say I'm a dirty boy."

"I love that you're a dirty boy. Dirty and HOT! You're the kind of guy I could take to a family picnic. While everyone is eating we sneak off behind some trees and get briefly crazy feeling each other up."

"Yep, that's me." Jagger says. "The guy's family prefers me than their actual son. I'm the one keeping it together and the one breaking away with you into the woods to rip your fucking clothes off. We'd have to bang away fast before anyone realizes were gone. Allow the sweat to drip down our bodies."

"I can tell that by looking at you. I was imagining as weird as it might sound, introducing you to my family and how they would say what a nice guy you are. I would slip away with you out of view and ravage every inch of your body. Nobody would ever know that we were getting off in the woods together." Trezner says moving in more on Jagger.

"I guess I have a way of drawing out the hot sex somehow. It's dangerous."

"Dangerous, but HOT! I love it. Keep drawing. I thought I was going to have to go home and pull out porn or something to get off, but being here with you is a thousand times better than any porn I could watch." Trezner professes.

"You have a live person screaming for your body here. It's not easy to say no or ignore that. Not if you're a hot-blooded dude. I've found it a little weird and ironic that people are excited to introduce me to their parents. They tell them about me and the parents fall in love. I'm saying, *'okay if you read some of my columns you'd be shocked it was the same person standing in front of you that you're so up in arms about'*. It's the art of seduction I guess. I don't know. Self examination maybe. I can't pinpoint it."

"I love the things I've read that you've written. You are descriptive with your words and your speech. It's a mind fuck. I can almost imagine you and me in the woods with sweat dripping off us as we go at it. Some of the things you say are direct. You're naked and raw when you talk. I'm in love with you." Trezner says.

"It's the little devil on my shoulder saying those things. I sometimes kick myself later for saying it or writing it."

"Don't ever regret what you write. I find it very sexy. I'm attracted to words and what people write bares much of their soul. I don't care what anybody says. You're a sweetheart and one sexy motherfucker. I was hoping that big fat cock of yours would help me celebrate. I'm comfortable around you now and not to mention the fact that you make me hornier than anybody I've ever met in my life."

Jagger smirks and pulls Trezner completely on him. They make out into fun foreplay for hours that leaves them both naked on each other.

Interestingly enough, Trezner vanished indefinitely after they parted at the end of the date. Jagger wasn't surprised. Where could it possible go? When they walked on the sidewalk Trezner was doing pop up wheelies off the curb with his skateboard. Jagger was mildly annoyed by it. He spent the date listening to Trezner's run down of how boys suck. He would nod and agree, but then reflect, *'but I always follow through.'* It was one of those things where you both mentally know that you'll be great acquaintances. Someone who you get along with while in each other's brief company, but when you've parted it's out of sight out of mind. You both know you're too different to even begin a relationship on any level. You may sleep together once or twice and have a silent respect for one other, but in the end there's that missing gap or link that would bind the two of you into something greater. On the other hand those acquaintance relationships sometimes last longer than close relationships or intense friendships. You run into them on and off over decades excited to see the other and not knowing why it doesn't build into anything. You have that great conversation for a bit and then you part once more for another three to six months only to pick up where you left off again. Trezner is twenty-two and one of Jagger's rules is the guy has to be at least twenty-five before he would even consider committing to him in a long term-relationship.

CHAPTER 10

Dude Habits

Sage was in town from New York City and hit Jagger up. He brought his wife Alora, the beautiful, hot, exotic blonde from Sweden.

Jagger wanted to sleep with both of them at the same time. "You still owe me dinner. Come on let's do it. It'll be perfectly innocent. What're you worried about?"

Sage laughs, "I don't think I could trust myself with you and that is not a good thing."

An interviewer once asked, '*You turn straight boys gay! What do you think that's all about?*'

Jagger smiled with nothing much to say on the matter. "I have no idea. I don't turn anyone in any direction that they don't already want to be in. I also don't believe in the illusion of turning straight guys gay. Sexuality is not all black and white despite popular myth."

Some tend to explore the idea a little or joke around, but they wouldn't go through with it. You're attracted to who you're attracted to. You don't know why. Enough with the labels and trying to figure it out.

With Jagger, the ability to explore on a verbal level with them is set up because they know they're safe with him. It's okay to bring out their fantasies or their secrets with him. They see a guy that feels like a close pal to them and that's what is attracting them in before anything else. It's Jagger's personality that they're drawn to. They can't help but fantasize about what it would be like. They all fantasize, but rarely admit it to the outside world. Jagger creates a safety net with people. He's downright charming when his guard is down. You can tell him anything, yet there is a huge amount of normalcy with him. Boys want to release energies together like they did as a kid that they deny when they're older. They can stroke it and be fully understood by another guy when doing that. Jagger doesn't invite it in. They open up the topic of discussion with him and he follows. He's a natural psychologist with a compassionate ear. Others find it easy to turn to him with their thoughts. His energy inspires trust and confession. Boys will be boys, unruly on the field and rowdy in the bedroom. Boys jack off together growing up regardless of their sexual preference. It's releasing those boyhood energies together. Our evolution is shifting. Boy energy is becoming more accepted and growing at an increased rate.

BUDDIES FOR LIFE

At a popular club by the beach, Jagger and Slade make their way through the crowd. Slade leans into Jagger's ear, "I told you. Isn't this great? Much better than staying home and feeling sorry for yourself. Skater boy is not worth your thoughts."

"You're such a powerful friend. You're always backing me up and cheering me on."

"You know it, Jagger." Slade reaches his arm around him as they walk through the club, "I'll stop in the middle of fucking a guy to come to your rescue whenever I hear that moving heartbreak in your voice. You are my Svengali man! No matter what happens or whoever we are with and whether or not that ends – we both know that we'll always go through it together. I love you buddy." Slade plants a kiss on Jagger's forehead.

Jagger knows he can count on Slade. He knows Slade sees him as something beyond just another guy.

At Russell's house, Slade was partying up with two half naked boys in Russell's pool. Slade and the other two boys formed a three way kiss in a huddle. Russell appeared closing the sliding door wearing shorts and a t-shirt. Slade stops kissing the other boys worried when he sees Russell's face. He moves away from the other boys and over to Russell who is solemn and down.

"What's up?" Slade asks.

"Edward left." Russell explains depressed, "It's over."

Slade's eyes fill with rare emotion.

"Where's Jagger?" Russell asks, "I need to talk to him."

"I haven't heard from him today." Slade says wishing Jagger were there since he would know what to do and what to say.

Garth surfs the waves of the now empty beach. The sun is setting and most of the beach goers have gone home. He enjoys this moment of silent, spiritual bliss.

CHAPTER 11

The Englishman

Piper is an English guy who is twenty-nine years old, but looks a bit older than that. He has that distinguished thing going. He could pass for mid-thirties. His hair is about shoulder length and falls freely over his face. He recently came back from a trip from Rome, Valencia and London. He is introduced to Jagger at Amanda's party. Piper is immediately enamored by Jagger's outer beauty instead of his inner hood.

"Do you believe in coincidences?" Piper asks moving behind Jagger at the party bar.

"Always." Jagger says uninterested.

"I had a press kit on my desk that had many samples of your columns."

Jagger takes a step back to get a good look at Piper. "So much for anonymity. That is trippy."

"We haven't met before have we?" Piper beams at him.

"Not that I know of."

"Only one way to find out." He flirts hoping to nail Jagger. "You're stunning. I love exotic features." Piper can't stop staring at him. When Jagger addresses him, Piper isn't listening and cuts him off. "I love your eyes. You're dead sexy."

Jagger pauses giving a low humble thanks and continues with his narrative, but then gets cut off again.

"I don't hit on that many guys since I'm a picky dude." Piper explains.

This captures Jagger's attention. Any guy who isn't out there talking to every guy with a cock in hopes to get some of it has a forceful chance at seizing Jagger's awareness. "There's nothing wrong with quality over quantity." Jagger softens wanting to make sure Piper knows he has his attention.

They stand awkward and silent. Piper looks around with vague aloofness assuming that Jagger moved on. It does tend to be the norm with most anyway in the modern day dating world. They contain a small attention span and become bored easily. They walk away and start talking to someone else. This is why dating apps, hook up apps, the media and social networking are a big contributor to the downfall of long term relationships as we know it.

Piper isn't done here though. "So you good? Life good?", and he goes for it, "I'd like to see you outside of this party, what do you think of that?"

"Hmm, okay, we can do that."

"Great! Here...." Piper pulls out his business card and a pen jotting his personal number on the back and handing it to him.

Jagger looks at the number and pulls out his own pen. He writes something on the back of the card. "Here you go. My number. Give me a call." He hands the card back with Piper's number crossed off and his in place instead. He had enough of being handed phone numbers from people who never call back. If Piper wants him, then let him prove it.

Three hours later when Jagger is back home he's alerted by his cell phone ringing. It is Piper. He heard that English accent speaking to him and he fell hard for it.

The Piper dude didn't waste any time. "Are you around this weekend?"

"Why? Did you want to get together?"

"YES!" Piper is excited. "Was I being too subtle?"

"Now that you mention it, I figured you were toying dangerously around the fringes of what you want."

Piper laughs loudly loving it.

"Our meeting will be strictly personal and not business." Jagger takes back the control.

"Hell yes!" Piper is hungry for him. "So sexy, what are you up to tomorrow?"

"Chilling." Jagger says.

"Maybe we could chill together?"

"Are you being subtle?" Jagger asks him.

"I'm British I can't help it."

"Europeans are the best. I have ancestors all over Europe, so I have European blood in me."

"Won't hurt to have a bit more in you. I can't wait to see those sexy eyes again." Piper offers.

"You're a poet!"

"A gentleman, a scholar, and a lover."

"A killer combo." Jagger smiles.

"That'll be for you to be the judge. I'm rather good with my hands by the way." Piper continues correcting himself from his tease, "Writing letters that is."

"We shall see if you truly are." Jagger tempts him.

The next day Piper calls Jagger asking him what he is up to.

"I'm supposed to hang with this guy named Piper." Jagger says.

Piper laughs, "Well what time should we walk together?"

"Now." Jagger says loving the romance that the guy conveys.

Piper in his very English diction spits out, "Lovely."

Piper said he will jog in the meantime while he waits for Jagger.

Anybody who cares about their health and their body is a favorable feature in Jagger's eyes. Jagger's been physically health conscious and attracted to mind, body, spirit awareness exercises more than anything. He's very sensitive to any discomfort or signals that his body gives him. He's definitely fussy about what he puts in his body.

Jagger heads to Piper's home in the posh Beverly Hills city. He calls Piper from the car minutes after he promised.

Piper answers his phone sleepy and with a tease. "You're late. I took a nap and didn't run after all."

"I let you sleep in on purpose so you can be well rested for me."

"You have beautiful eyes and a cool smile." Piper adds, "Have I said that to you yet?"

Jagger knows he can get used to his constant complimenting. "I'll never get tired of hearing it."

Jagger reaches the front door of Piper's place. A big black dog jumps excitedly up and down when Piper opens the door to his Rodeo Drive pad. Jagger mumbles, "Ah shit, a dog. Better not jump on me."

Jagger attempts to walk past the dog and to the brown antique wooden dining table that is placed perfectly next to a large window. He throws his keys on it, pulls his big black sunglasses off and sets them on the table. Piper takes a step back and smiles leering into his eyes. "Whoa. More intense than I remembered the other night."

Jagger smirks.

Piper's place is impeccably decorated with fine art on the walls. Roman and Greek statues adorn the living room. Only the best and most classy couches and chairs carefully bought. A bottle of hard liquor sits on the clean and clutter-*less* kitchen counter top.

"How about we go out onto the patio outside and talk. It's a beautiful day with a beautiful guy." Piper advises.

Jagger nods and follows him out onto the patio. They sit down and gaze at each other up and down absorbing the strong attraction. Piper's relaxed expensive looking brown sweat pants and his button up shirt halfway reveal part of his sexy chest. His slightly nervous demeanor in Jagger's presence makes him all hot inside. The excessively decorated, proper, prim man had a naughty, bad boy in his home.

Another little dog shows up and wraps himself quietly under Jagger's chair. The dog had been sick and homeless. Piper found it and had been trying to find him a home. For the past two months his place has been the dog's home.

Jagger says, "You take in strays too. Sweet."

"Yeah they keep me grounded. They sleep in the bed with me."

"They do? Isn't that unsanitary or slightly twisted?" Jagger asks.

"Hmm. It might be." Piper chuckles nervously.

"I love animals, but they will not sleep in my bed. They will have their own bed." Jagger insists, "Why does one need a relationship if they are already in one with their dog?"

"Well, when you're in my bed, I'll make sure it's just the two of us." Piper winks.

"You're pretty confident that this is going to lead to that, aren't ya?" Jagger is a tough audience.

Both dudes have matching black beach flip-flops on. Piper reaches his foot over and touches Jagger's with his for about half a second. The two speak for two hours straight absorbing each other as much as they can, smiling and laughing at the fated coincidences between them.

The dog is getting antsy. Fucking dog. Piper says he'd love Jagger's company if he would be interested in accompanying him to walk the dogs. Jagger agrees wanting to spend more time with Piper. They reach the sidewalk and Piper places his hand affectionately on Jagger's back. Jagger takes hold of the leash for one of the dogs. They both stroll on the sidewalk next to each other. They each walk a dog like two peas in a pod, two lovers and two for the road.

Thirty minutes later, they arrive back at Piper's place and talk for a little more on the patio. Piper sits back in his chair and throws on a smile. "What do you say our next step should be here?"

Jagger stumbles a little. "I'm not sure. What would you like to see happen?" The total infatuation high is taking over him.

Piper's hair falls over his face and he lifts it back up. "I'd like to see you again. Take you out to dinner. What do you think? We can progress slowly from there."

Jagger deliberates. *Progress into what?* He could never fit into this person's life and his lifestyle. This is a showy, upper-class man, who demands the utmost finest. Here he is making a pass at him as if he is a new prized trophy that he can place on his mantel next to the other beautiful ceramics in his home. And maybe, just maybe, he will take him down to play with once in a dear moment. He doesn't want to dismiss the obvious attraction between them though.

Piper's face lights up, "You do have a say in it too. You know if you want to." He isn't sure if Jagger is agreeing or not by his silence.

Jagger catches Piper's first glimpse of insecurity, so he reassures him. "Yes I want to!"

Piper laughs strolling with Jagger towards the door. They agree to call each other after the long Independence Day weekend that is coming up. Jagger puts his hand out. Piper grabs and hugs him instead.

"Oh we're at that stage already huh?" Jagger says.

Jagger heads down to his truck smiling a stupid smile he can't erase. He wants to tell the whole world about it, but pulls back instead not wanting to read too much into it too quickly.

He jots in his notepad: *'He'll find out what a reckless talker I am who almost immediately releases whatever pops into his head before thinking, yet loving my most broadminded and unnoticed by myself use of profanity. Troy is careful about his words. He's well spoken, yet I've caught him cursing under his breath during stress. Slade uses exaggeration, everything is the best everything. The best sex! The greatest fucking! He's loud and excited, while Russell is subdued, strong and calm. Even they can do much better here than me.'*

Slade drags Jagger to a club during the pride festivities. Jagger roams with him unimpressed, then he leans into Slade's ear, "No one dances anymore they only gyrate."

Guys are grinding with their shirts off and a chick dances on a little raised platform in the middle of the room. She has on a leather-bikini thing and very tight super short leather shorts. They are so tight that they aren't zipped up all the way. I suppose it's safe to say that she isn't dancing. She is simulating fucking for a few minutes while people watch in awe. Is that what Pride is all about? Sex. You go to a Greek Festival or Renaissance Fair and you have great food and history surrounding the theme of the Festival and Fair taking place. Pride festivals? Eh, not so much. It's thongs and shirtless people who are wasted trying to get laid.

Slade is in the right place of course as he nabs a bunch more phone numbers to add to his hook up list. Jagger signs boy's chests, abs, asses, and other places they'd be too drunk to remember. He feels a little down and let's Slade know he has to go home. He doesn't know why it has been a week and no word from Piper. Buttoning up and pulling himself together he decides to call him anyway.

Piper has full on English snobbery when he answers the phone. "Oh I just figured we weren't meant to be."

"What?" Jagger asks confused, "What are you talking about?" He doesn't know if he is kidding or being honest.

"I called you earlier in the week to let you know I had a great time and I didn't hear back from you."

Jagger has the phone pressed to his ear thinking back through his messages and not getting one from Piper. He remembers he was having cell phone issues days ago and maybe that's when he called. Fucking technology. "No, I enjoyed you and want to see you. Something was up with my phone and I lost messages, didn't get calls, it was a mess."

Piper is quiet and rudely distant. "Yeah, well if we tried again, we'd have to start over from the beginning and meet at the same place we met at the party. Who knows when another party we're both invited to will be at the same place."

Is this guy for real or what? What's with the attitude problem?

Jagger starts to speak, but realizes that Piper has hung up on him already. He looks at his phone to see the call has ended. He stands in the middle of the crowd thinking, analyzing, and trying to figure out what could've gone wrong. He recalls the guy's hair needed a wash. His accent and uncouth attitude should be buried in a coffin alive.

Slade has been watching him knowing it didn't go well. Jagger brushes past him running from hurt to anger unable to speak. A drunken guy approaches Jagger. "Hey, let's fuck."

Jagger grabs the guys face with his hand and shoves him back hard.

"Hey!" The drunk guy shouts.

"Maybe you should stop drinking." Slade tells the guy. He moves into a jog racing after Jagger.

The drunk guy screams, "Fucking jerk offs!"

Slade approaches Jagger. "What happened?"

"That asshole hung up on me." Jagger nods heated about to blow up at someone.

Jagger paces in his living room angry. Slade sits on his couch watching him. Troy stands near the corridor of the hall worried.

"I don't get it. I put myself out there again bare and naked and for what? I'm done with this." Jagger tells them.

"We should take his fucked up English ways and bury it alive." Slade suggests giving Jagger an idea.

"You read my mind." Jagger lights up with the idea of revenge. "Come on."

Jagger and Slade take off towards the front door.

Troy is alerted and runs after them. "Wait. Do what?"

"Get even." Jagger says.

Jagger, Slade and Troy climb into Jagger's truck and skid off down the street in a fury.

"So why are we doing this again?" Troy asks concerned.

Slade does not want to be held back. "You shouldn't have come if you're having second thoughts."

"I need my closure." Jagger explains, "I'm only speaking up about things that are important to me. Respect is one of them."

A barefoot homeless man walks down the side of the road with a blanket around him. He's in his early thirties and dirty. He hasn't been homeless for more than a year.

Jagger races down the main highway alongside the beach and notices the man. He skids his truck to a stop in the middle of the road without pulling over.

"There's a bag of groceries I left back there! Hand me that bag!" Jagger says to Troy urgently.

"You can't just stop in the middle of the road!" Troy slams back.

"Yes I can I just did! I need that bag please." Jagger shouts.

Troy grabs the bag and hands it to Jagger.

Jagger makes a U-turn and drives behind the homeless man and stops the truck. He hops out with the bag and jogs up behind the man and smiles.

"Hi. This is for you. There's food in this bag. I'm sorry, but it's all I have on me right now."

Jagger hands the man the bag of food. The man looks at the bag and then at Jagger. He takes the bag from him with sudden joy in his eyes. "Thank you."

Jagger smiles and nods, then jogs back to the truck and hops in. He whips another U-turn heading right back down towards his intended destination.

Slade and Troy look out their respective windows thinking about the rare act of kindness they witnessed by man.

Jagger pulls up on the dark street where Piper lives. He, Slade and Troy all file out of the truck. Troy hangs back watching Jagger and Slade moving briskly over to Piper's car.

Slade then heads over to Piper's front balcony and unzips his pants and begins peeing.

Jagger whips a blade out of his back pocket and slashes one of Piper's tires.

Troy is panicked and wants them to hurry now that he's seen what they're up to. He heads over to Jagger and stands behind him as he slashes another tire.

"It's my heart." Jagger says with ruthless anger as another slice of the final tire happens. "Next time. Murder."

Slade jogs back to the truck and pulls out an American flag. He tosses it to Jagger who drapes it on Piper's car pleased.

"I. Was. Here." Jagger smiles deviously, which scares Troy.

"Okay, let's get out of here." Troy says urging them to move quickly in a panic.

"Feel better?" Slade asks Jagger.

"Much better." Jagger says satisfied.

"Good. Let's go."

All three of them head back to the truck. Slade pats Troy on the back. "He's just fighting back kid. Standing his ground for all of us."

They all climb back in the truck and Jagger races off down the highway along the beach back home.

"I thought England was supposed to be the country of manners." Slade asks him.

"Bad manners with this one. He doesn't represent the country well or humanity for that matter." Jagger says.

"What if he calls the police and knows it was us?" Troy is still panicked.

"He won't." Jagger says sure of himself, "The fuckwad will be too chicken shit to do anything. This was his warning. I'll be much worse next time. I'll just tell the police it was self-defense. He hurt me first. If we don't make things happen, then they happen to us. Sense the betrayal, the delicious satisfaction of brilliantly designed revenge? I can. It's better than any drink I've ever sipped."

"This Piper dude isn't worth the paper he's printed on. He has no value." Slade tells Troy.

"Why do you think he got weird like that all of a sudden?" Troy asks.

"That's easy. He was always weird to begin with. I just didn't know him. It's easier to replace a sex object than it is to replace an object of love." Jagger clarifies.

Jagger was outraged by having to go through another dramatic exchange with a potential suitor. He let it out in his column as he typically does. The more he lashed out in his column the more popular he and it would grow to become. After Piper, he was inspired to criticize those who have an obsession with dogs in his next column:

"I love dogs. I just don't want to sleep with them. Relationships break up over dogs. Manywho sleep in the same bed with their dogs tend to have a difficult time in keeping long term love relationships going. It's easier to thrive in a relationship with a dog, because the dog gives you unconditional love without question and doesn't talk back. Matthew and April had been dating for a few months when the reality slowly sunk in for Matthew. He wanted to go away with April one weekend, but April couldn't leave her dog at home. They

ended up going nowhere. Another night after their date, he asked April to finally spend the night at his place because she never did. Her response was, "I can't. Rufus is waiting for me at home." When she offered an alternative that he spend the night at her place, he jumped at the idea. His excitement soon evaporated when April's dog climbed into bed with her. She put her arms around the dog instead. Matthew soon realized that April was seeing someone else. Her dog. Matthew left in the middle of the night and never returned."

CHAPTER 12

The Professor

Jagger needed time to withdraw and re-center his energies that had been knocked off balance by allowing himself to get close to Piper. It was late in the evening when he pulled out the motorcycle he never uses out of his garage and revved it up. An old lady who was walking down the sidewalk jumped out of the way startled, but he didn't care. He took off down to Pacific Coast Highway winding around the ocean at a raging speed with his rock music blaring into his earpiece in his helmet.

The next day he lay down on his bed burying his head in the sand. He couldn't seem to get up out of his slump, It's much better to dig your heels in and start to work on those things that you know deep down need work. You can waste time wondering what it was you did wrong which is what Jagger did. He didn't want to move, but instead pathetically mourn another loss.

Slade approached Jagger's front door and knocked on it for a few minutes. He jumped onto the nearby tree and clawed his way up barely latching onto the side of the balcony. He pulled himself over the balcony and jumped in. He walked into Jagger's place through the balcony door that was wide open for any intruder. He saw Jagger sleeping in the bed. "Okay that's it! Time to get up. It's Noon."

Jagger cut in and out of sleep. "No."

Slade jumps on the bed and climbs over him. "Come on, sexy." He smacks his ass. "You are in the bell jar my friend. I'm getting you out of here. You got to get back on the horse."

"Nope."

Slade hovers over him. "There are too many people relying on you. Can't you hear your troops outside your balcony? What are they supposed to think if they find out you're in here sipping beer and watching a film when you should be out their planning and strategizing?"

"They'll get over it." Jagger says with his head buried in his pillow.

"Come on! You'll feel better when you do what you were trained to do."

"By who?"

"By God! Gees man! Let's go!" He pulls Jagger up. "Shall I climb in the shower with you or...."

"I got it. I got it. Sly boy."

"Just once, you need my help this morning anyway. I've already seen you naked before. Hell everybody has at this point."

Jagger shoots him a look with a smirk.

Later that night at a party in Hermosa Beach, Jagger discovered he didn't need much alcohol to be spirited. He knows Slade is right to let those moonbeams do their job. He is good at perfecting that smile and walking away.

"Jagger!" Troy is a little tipsy from the alcohol, "If it weren't for you I'd jump off a bridge." Troy grabs Jagger and wraps his arms around him.

Slade leans in against the bar with Tiki everything dangling from it. He collects three shots and hands them to Jagger and Troy.

Troy suggests that maybe Jagger better let go of the English bastard and face the fact that regardless of his background that dogs come in all shapes and sizes. Who knows what you might find. The three of them clinked each other's shot glasses and threw the alcohol back into their mouths simultaneously slamming them all down one by one onto the bar.

"Mmm. Ah shit, I'll be right back." Jagger takes off through the crowd.

A tall handsome guy walks past him with a smile. "Hey bud, aren't you damn sexy. Love that body. Cute ass and that sexy face, overall you have a hot sexy look! You're definitely all 10's from me man!"

Jagger gives off his signature strong, arctic gawk. He shakes his head and mumbles walking away. "Sweet."

"That's it?" The guy can't stop smiling. His hands open in the air with a come hither look. "How about you go out with me?"

"Why?" Jagger is officially dead and not falling for it again. He takes off through the crowd.

The guy jogs up to him. "Whoa-whoa-whoa seriously. Wait, hang on." He jots his number down quick, "Call me. I'm Nevada and I swear I'm a good boy."

Jagger looks up at him, "Nevada? Sure you are."

Nevada oozes sweetness and is almost innocent. Jagger reaches over to take the folded piece of paper with the guy's number on it. "Okay, Nevada I'll call you."

"Right on. Damn. What's your name?"

Jagger smiles a little and walks away through the crowd. He pauses, then says to Nevada, "Jagger."

Nevada beats his chest a few times with his fist. "Call quickly!"

Jagger mumbles to himself. "Shit what am I doing?"

Jagger surfs on a wave of optimism and is ready to climb right back out of his hole for more. He knows crossing this ocean of life is nothing but a breeze with the occasional iceberg in his path. This time when he sees those large masses of ice in his way, he'll swim around them instead of at them.

After a phone call and flirtatious conversation, Nevada asks Jagger out on a date. He wants to romance him first before he gets him into bed.

"Where are you?" Nevada asks.

"I'm wandering around near the beach."

"Oh yeah, working the boulevard?"

"Yes, I am on the street that runs alongside the beach." Jagger looks around amazed at his accuracy.

"I'll buy you baby that way you never have to work again."

"Oh yeah? My mom warned me about boys like you."

"Interesting, since mine warned me about boys like you. Too hot to touch." Nevada says keeping up the flirtation.

Nevada is a professor at the local university where he teaches Algebra. He is 35 years old, blue eyes, dark hair and a fox with a killer smile. Jagger is afraid to let him know what type of writing he does. The guy may ask him to leave. He's acceptable and presentable, a real low-key chivalry man on a white horse. Jagger knows he'd only dent his intellectual world with his sex talk. He had to answer him truthfully regardless. He can't lie to save his life and they find out the truth in the end anyway.

"I write about love and relationships." Jagger explained, "I analyze in my head to death why people act a certain way with someone they don't know." Jagger mumbled feeling like a complete benign idiot.

Nevada loves it regardless. "I'm impressed. I want to take you out tonight. Anywhere you want to go."

Jagger begs him to challenge him so it'll help him with his next column. "Dump me so I can write about it."

Nevada says, "I was with a guy who cheated on me and he wasn't a very good person. He used to tell me when and where we were going for dinner."

"He had the upper hand and was probably older." Jagger suggests.

When a guy takes you out, he wants sex with you at some point. Most likely sooner than later, but if it can be held out for at least three dates of long erotic making out, then watch out for those amazing fireworks when the clothes are finally peeled off and you're fucking away later.

At the outdoor promenade, Nevada wants to see a movie. Jagger isn't too keen on the idea. He sees expressed disappointment in Nevada's eyes. Nevada looks away almost angry, like a child who had been told they weren't going to get any candy. Jagger studies him for a moment. He doesn't want him to think it has anything to do with him not being interested because he is. He remembered the last time he had a movie crises with someone by the name of Caden and knows how that turned out.

Jagger places his hand tenderly on Nevada's stomach and runs it up the center of his chest. His face moves in forward into Nevada's left ear. He is invading his personal space taking it over. His lips reach Nevada's ear ready to suck on it like it's a strawberry. His lips open slowly imagining for a brief second what it would be like to have Nevada's lips and never let go. The words come out sure of themselves. They are firm in its most sexy low recording blues voice. "I don't want to spend two hours facing forward when that's time I can be using to be alone with you." Jagger pulls his face back out of Nevada's vicinity and releases his hand from the guy's chest. He takes a step backward out of his personal circle.

Nevada's smile is pasted wide like a horny teenager experiencing his first time. "Oh we're going to do that. Trust me. That's a given!" He is excited and sure of himself.

Jagger smiles knowing he has some control in this too. "Good. Let's go get our tickets."

The movie previews were showing cartoons like they used to do in the 1950's. Nevada bursts out laughing extremely loud at the hi-jinx on the screen. Another minute passes and he lets out a second loud roar of laughter fly out of his mouth. Jagger's eyes widen almost embarrassed. He looks slightly over at him not thinking the cartoon is funny at all. "Shit. Dude."

Nevada taps Jagger's foot with his in affection. The mating birds calling. During the film, he puckers up a simulated kiss with his lips from afar. He leans over to Jagger during the film to whisper, "Kiss me."

"No. Wait until the movie is done." Jagger is attempting to be a good little boy, but he wants to taste Nevada fucking badly.

"I'm going to keep asking until you do it." He smiles.

"Fine. Keep asking."

When they get up Nevada mumbles something. Jagger thinks he is asking what he thought about the movie. "Oh it was great! I loved it."

Nevada laughs, "Huh? No, I was saying that I admired your ass."

"Oh."

Back at the car, they are grid locked in. Nevada can't take it anymore. He leans in a little to Jagger. "Hey."

"Hey." Jagger is a little uncomfortable, but excited.

Nevada moves in for the kill. His kiss starts a fire. Long. Hot. Wet. Jagger grows a boner.

When fate has forced you to be with an attractive stranger for a brief second, why do you start looking around at everything else except the attractive stranger?

The next day, Jagger is too in shock to say anything when he bumps into Garth on the beach. Jagger is preoccupied with playing with his phone only to discover Garth is right there in front of him with his surfboard under his arm. Jagger can tell when someone looks at him a certain way how into him they are. Garth's face is serious and he just glares at Jagger. There is no one else around them for a change, yet neither can say a word to the other. Jagger continues on his walk back home. Garth is heading the other way onto the beach. He stops to let Jagger pass him. He looks away and down at the pavement coyly as they brush past one another.

As Jagger slinks past him, he thinks, 'oh my god he IS into me.' He suddenly feels guilty as if he is cheating on Garth. It's the look that Garth gives him that says,'How could you?' They're both connected in a soul karmic thread that they can *feel* what's going on without knowing each other. Jagger wonders if he's the one again and that he shouldn't dabble with Nevada this intensely as it will only delay the connection with Garth. It could lead to something serious and fate has cast he and Garth in the roles, not anyone else.

Jagger is the typical confused male, but strong boy searching for love. He plops himself on his bed with his headphones on low, zoning out to the music that begins to grow louder as he drifts off into a nap. He floats in his dreams to Russell's place in the warm Jacuzzi watching the bubbles evaporate into steam. A pair of hands land on his legs. The water morphs into an animation cartoon. Garth is under the water as a cartoon character kissing Jagger's stomach and planting them up Jagger's body and bare chest.

Garth's face rises out from underneath the water to place his lips erotically onto Jagger's. Both of their eyes are closed and everything goes black moments before their lips hit.

Jagger opens his eyes. He is lying on his bed facing the ceiling. He is alone and it never happened. He feels low and suffocated as if he can't breathe without him. It's Garth he dreams about, not Nevada or anybody else.

The next day, Nevada is distant and pulls away from Jagger.

"What's up?" Jagger asks.

"What's up with us?" Nevada says, "I mean you're fucking hot and all I think about is getting you naked and being with you sexually and intimately...."

Jagger interrupts understanding where he is going with it. "But where could this possibly go is your point. Where can lust void of anything else go between two people?"

Nevada nods agreeing.

"If you say that, then you're thinking in a limited way. I like you beyond the sex. If you asked me if I liked you and could see myself exclusively dating you, then I'd say yes no questions asked."

Jagger backs up against the wall and crosses his arms guarded on offense and irritated. Nevada walks up to him not being able to stand it anymore and kisses him some more.

He asks Jagger when he can see him again. Jagger says irritated that he brought up reservations, "Whenever you want."

"How about tomorrow?" Nevada asks.

"Sounds good. I'll call you tomorrow then."

The next day Jagger calls Nevada up. Nevada says he is on his way to Bakersfield to spend some time with his parents on their ranch.

Jagger wonders, '*Why say you want to see me and then make other plans? That makes no sense.*' He lets it go, as he's also a believer that things come up and it's not his business except to be understanding and then make the plans for another day. Still – something wasn't right about that.

Nevada offered, "You want to get together tomorrow night after I get back?"

Jagger thought why not. He was asked to call him the next day. He called like clockwork leaving him a hello message.

A week passed and no returned call. *Fuck him.* It doesn't take someone seven days to call you back. Kick him to the curb.

Where do you find a decent man? They say you won't find him in any boys town anywhere in the universe, nor on any buddy sex app. The dismal and unfortunate thing is many out there look in those places. They believe because there are so many choices, they'll find one. But the problem is you're dealing with a candy store of short attention spans. They have hopes of wrangling a buck to be their soul mate. Wherever there is a place that is invaded by others like yourself the odds are extreme and against you. You have hundreds of guys all there for the same thing. It's a sexual brothel and the competition is everywhere. Maybe you'll find him there, but you won't keep him past two weeks let alone a couple days. He'll be off and running around with a new boy that'll lead to a secret sexual rendezvous. You'll be forced to move on and do the same. Before you know it, years have gone by. It's become your life and you've never felt this alone. You hurt for a day maybe a couple more. You push yourself to move on after the first night because enough is enough. He's not worth your thoughts. This isn't to say that real love doesn't live right there in the heart of it all. You dig under the haystack to find the one jewel that stands out.

Boys town is a place that the media investigates to heavily portray in media entertainment, but what is disheartening is that's only one percent of the rest of the world. Those that exist in that life are a small percentage. It's not the whole picture. They never branch out to see the other shades that survive because those shades aren't as obvious and exaggerated. They're the Wall Street brokers, the lawyers, doctors, and surfers. They blend in with the rest of the world. The percentage of their existence is much greater because it's not concentrated in one area, but rather they're all over the world with varied interests. They blend in with each other and not because of fear, but because it's who they are. It's how they were born. They are regular people whose driving force is not who is in their bedroom. It's their integrity and what they set out to do. Their sexuality and preference isn't what pushes them forward. If Hollywood is going to make a movie about someone like this, they want him to be the larger-than-life character that we know to be in boy's town. They're not telling the whole truth when they do that. Show all of them or don't bother.

Another week had passed and no word from Nevada. If you take longer than a couple of days you're already off his list. Jagger is distraught wandering the sidewalks with no destination planned. He picks up his phone and starts to dial it.

"Hey Russell, it's Jagger. I thought you might like to know that Bambi is following me. She has blonde-blonde hair, huge sunglasses, big boobs, red bell-bottoms and huge red heels. I'm not sure what she wants, but all I know is that I'm not in the fucking mood. Where are you?" He pulls the phone away from his ear ready to hang up and brings the phone back to his mouth. "Fuck." He sighs, "Call me. I've had sex with four different people this past week, Karen on Thursday, Sam on Friday, Sheryl on Saturday, and Richard on Sunday. I need some desperate intervention. I've felt nothing with all of them. I'm officially a whore. I'm....oh my God. I'm Slade!"

Jagger knows he should sever all ties with these people and be with someone of substance.

Russell calls Jagger back. "If you're with someone that is holding you back from being with the person you belong with, then you need to break it off. This Nevada guy is another bad spec. You know he's not the one for you. You know who that guy is. You just have to talk to him already."

"I know. You're right." Jagger says, "I listened to this guy on the radio talk about how he fell in love with another guy. They've been together for a year and now he wants a family. The guy is on the road and he misses him when he's gone. I wasn't buying it. I caught myself daydreaming about how it won't be long before they split up. I'm getting angrier and I can't stop it. It's erupting uncontrollably."

Slade intervenes again. He won't allow Jagger to hide out in his cocoon for too long. It's not his style and nor is it Jagger's. He's been consistent on getting back on track. Slade takes Jagger to a crowded restaurant/bar near the beach. While leaning against the bar, Jagger notices something that jars him.

"Oh I don't believe this bullshit here." Jagger points him out, "That's Nevada right over there. Looks like he's on a date with someone."

Slade looks around. "What! No way."

"I'll be right back." Jagger picks up his drink and pushes his way through the crowd. Slade gets up smiling knowing this is going to get good. Nevada's eyes widen seeing the beauty that is Jagger approaching him, but he just as quickly gets nervous knowing he's in for it.

"Hi. Jagger. I was..." Nevada starts to speak.

Jagger whips his drink into Nevada's mouth and all over him.

"Whoops." Jagger slams the glass on the table.

"Dammit!" Nevada attempts to compose himself.

Jagger is full of rage scooping up the food off Nevada's plate and flinging it into Nevada's face. The tables around them and Nevada's date all gasp in horror. Slade laughs uncontrollably smacking his hands together.

"Break it off with me before you start dating someone else ass wipe." Jagger says.

Nevada attempts to stand up to fight, but his elbow hits his plate knocking the rest of the food on his lap. Jagger grabs Nevada's dinner napkin and flings it at him. "Here ya go."

Slade grabs Jagger and ushers him away. "Let's go buddy."

They push through the crowd of shocked and smiling onlookers and head out the door.

"Shit!" Nevada stands up, but before he can gain composure Jagger and Slade have vanished.

CHAPTER 13

Beached Hut Blues

As upset as Jagger is with Nevada and all the previous dudes lumped together, it quickly diminishes when he sees a clan of hundreds of kids and adults march holding a banner that says: *"Community for peace."* Jagger crosses the street to the beach. Our problems are not as bad when compared to the bigger issues going on in the world.

Jagger reaches the sand on the beach and sits down defeated.

He suddenly notices Garth standing not that far from him. Garth is at attention with his hands in his pockets. His feet push themselves into the sand. He looks out at the people in the ocean. The wind blows through his dirty blonde hair. His blondish-brown hair on his arms and legs reflect under the sun like diamonds. He turns around and sees Jagger who looks away as if he is uninterested. Jagger considers that maybe the one that's been for him all along has been sitting right in front of him this whole time again. Neither of them will say or do anything about it.

Two surfers race passed Garth and into the water on their surfboards. Danny, another surfer hangs behind and stops next to Garth.

"You like him." Danny says as a matter of fact.

"What are you talking about?" Garth is thrown off balance.

"It's cute, but that guy is unobtainable. He is a catch if you can nab him though. Sexy as hell if it's guys you're into."

"Maybe I want to work for someone's affections for a change." Garth says.

Danny nods with a smile. "Right. Go for it. What do you have to lose?"

Garth looks over at Jagger in the distance.

"Talk to him." Danny smiles, "Wanna grab your board and join us?"

"Alright mate." Garth jogs slowly back to his lifeguard hut behind him. He pulls his surfboard out and takes it out into the ocean. Paddling out into the ocean he glances back to shore at the foot of the sand. He watches Jagger walking along the path towards the promenade.

Jagger allows his thoughts to wander as he contemplates. *'Sometimes it's best to make peace with the past and give yourself permission to move forward. There are new exploits that are being prepared to come your way. You can't let regrets about the past haunt you. If only I could be Garth's Prince for a day. What a day that would be!'*

Garth carves out on a huge wave owning it. The wave carries him back to shore with amazing ease. He jumps off his board and jogs back to the lifeguard hut and dries off. He locks it up and heads down the path where Jagger was twenty minutes before.

Jagger strolls down the boardwalk next to the promenade with the strip of shops, restaurants, bars and clubs alongside it. He walks into the Beached Hut that is fully open to the wind and the beach. He sits on the table outside with his huge signature dark sunglasses. A waiter sets down a cold beer and some hookah even though he doesn't smoke, but today he will be.

Jagger relaxes into his chair when he hears a voice behind him. "You've had many bad relationships haven't you?"

"Is it that obvious?" Jagger adjusts and is surprised to see Trezner. "Hey."

Trezner smiles and sits down at the table with Jagger. "I get a vibe off you. You push me away when I try to get close." He rubs his forehead a little.

"I do?" Jagger looks out at the people having a good time on the beach puzzled. The waiter sets a cold beer next to Trezner.

"I think about you often. I can be having the shittiest day and when I talk to you or see you, then I light up. Even if my day is going good, it's much better afterwards."

Trezner glides his hand across Jagger's arm to the hookah cigarette between Jagger's fingers. He takes it and brings it up to his lips to inhale a little blowing it out. "I didn't know you smoke."

"I don't. It's been a shitty summer." He winks sympathetically at Trezner. "I didn't know you still smoke."

"Me, nah, I don't either." Trezner's grin widens.

"I'm surprised you're here." Jagger says.

"I should've called you and I didn't. I wanted to. I have got shit going on in my head."

"We all do."

"I know a lot more than you think I do." Trezner confesses, "I know about a certain someone here on this beach that you like. Don't let a guy bring you down. You've been stronger than that paving the way for people like me. I haven't deleted that one voicemail you left me a couple months ago. That way I can hear your voice whenever I want." He stretches his arms out making fists with his hands and back down to grab his cold one taking a sip. "And damn! I would love more than anything to cuddle with you again and to have your arms around me, more than the hot sex we would have." He winks.

"Humph." Jagger smiles a little nodding already knowing he was into him. His confession is proof. "I know."

"I've thought your eyes were killer! I was sucked right into you when I first saw you and that slight smile. It was warm, strong and sweet in the kindest way. I mean come on! Would I lie to you to get in your jeans?"

Jagger shoots a look that says, '*well, what do you think?*'

Trezner laughs, "Well, maybe! I was sure that you were my kind of guy. You're sexy."

"No, I'm not."

"Yes, you are." Trezner insists.

"You need to stop putting me on a pedestal."

"You belong on a pedestal."

"Whatever you say playboy. Beauty fades." Jagger assures him.

"You should come with me to this hot new club that's opened up. They're having a strip contest. Maybe you could enter?"

"What is it, Chippendales? Besides I've done enough stripping for one year." Jagger shoots more of his drink in him setting it on the table. "I realize how much I mean to you. I didn't grasp it before."

"You do mean a lot to me. I've had trouble figuring out what it is I want and what I want to do. My problem is there are 101 things I know I could do and would enjoy, but I'm scared of committing to one thing that I end up committing to nothing. Though I imagine it's coming. It's coming up on the horizon." He gestures ahead at the radiant sunset lighting up the sky.

Jagger's eyebrows stay arched blowing his smoke away from Trezner. He smashes the butts into the tray in front of him. "I don't know why I'm smoking this." He places his complete focus on Trezner. "You're not ready and that's okay. When you know what your place is and what you want, and you know that you will never stop until you get there, then you'll be perfectly happy to commit. You'll find something that'll make you happy, and if it doesn't then back out and move to the next thing until you find the thing that will."

Trezner's eyes widen and he leans in close wanting to listen. He hopes to catch a little of that magic off Jagger's message.

Jagger continues, "Maybe you don't like to be confined? Maybe you'd be great with something where you can travel or move about. Something in communications or where you can use your words. People will eat out of your hands with that and your good looks." Jagger shakes his head, gives a whistle that says fuck, damn. "The killer combo that is sure to give you what you want."

Jagger has a way with making people feel at ease using his vocabulary. He can make them fall in love with him if they hadn't already.

Trezner chokes for a second. "No one's ever said that to me. That's probably the most inspiring thing I've heard and most cherished gift you've given to me. My mind goes through a work out with you. Your words and meaning can be complex."

Jagger is pleased that he can make someone happy. He stands up and rests his hand on Trezner's shoulder. "Good." He reaches over and kisses his cheek. "I should get going. Thank you."

Trezner gets up grabbing his skateboard. "I'll be keeping my eye on you."

Jagger smirks a little. "You better."

"Oh and hey Jagger." Trezner rises grabbing his skateboard, "We both know who you're meant to be with." He gestures inside and slams his skateboard down and takes off. Jagger watches him take off confused, until he notices Garth inside. He walks back inside noticing the crowd has increased. He is distraught and no smiles on his face anymore, no dancing eyes, only an icy gaze.

Garth sits up on the counter with a few beach people talking. He looks at Jagger and his mouth opens, *'there he is.'* He quickly jumps down nervously wanting to make a move, but too many people around now. Jagger says nothing as usual, but a silent acknowledgement. He dare not let on that he has a big crush on him or he'd die of embarrassment. It'll be easier for him to be butt naked in public than say hello to this man.

Jagger relies on his friends to prop him back up including his brother, Jameson. Jameson is a stuntman in films. They throw back some beer and kick back. Men love to drink beer with each other. It's a bonding ritual. It relieves stress from the everyday pressures of life. Jagger asks him what happened between him and the girl he was seeing.

"We broke up." Jameson says.

"Why, what happened?"

"We don't agree on the same things. She's that typical Jewish American Princess."

Jagger is aghast, "Oh, say no more I get it."

"It was passionate, but..."

"That fades if you don't have other things in common." Jagger explains.

"Yeah, she wanted to be pampered with things and I can't do that. I'm a survivor." Jameson takes another swig of his beer. "You and I are both survivors from the same bad place and we can't be with people like that."

Jagger looks away with a detached scowl understanding how true it is.

"What about you? Still like that lifeguard?" Jameson smiles.

"Is there anybody who doesn't know about this?" Jagger chuckles, "You're doing much better than I am in the love department, let me say that."

"You got to make the move bro."

"I don't know about that. He's got to do it or it's not happening. I'm over this bad summer of love and don't know how much more I can take of this. I never press the rewind button. Once I'm done with you, I'm done. I put you in the recycle bin. You know how you put something out in that blue recycle can outside your house? You later find that someone pulled some of that shit out of it as if it were gold. It isn't long afterwards before they've taken that recycled material home only to discover that something is wrong with it. This is the reason it was thrown in the bin to begin with."

CHAPTER 14

Endless Summer

Jagger heads down to the beach wearing his board shorts and holding his surfboard under his arm. He stands against the railing that divides the sand from the pavement path under the hot beating sun. He isn't sure if he wants to surf, sit on the sand, wait for the sun to set or people watch. He knows he wants to be closer to God so he looks out on the gorgeous blue ocean reflecting on it. Because the waves are not that high today, the scads of surfers sit on their boards instead. They wait for the right wave to reveal itself. There is an older man in his late fifties who is taking his time drying off near the outdoor showers. The squeak of a door of the main lifeguard house that is built of bricks next to it badly needing some oil rings in Jagger's ear.

The man drying off speaks. "Oh, hey Garth. How are you?"

Jagger's heart falls into his chest wanting to die when he hears Garth's name. He's paralyzed, but brings himself to attention. He needs to sneak a glance without being obvious.

The old man continues, "You've been working out here on the beach a lot, working many hours, keeping busy. Are you running things here yet?"

Garth's voice rings in Jagger's ears long enough to hear. It scratches like a recording of the best music. Jagger loves his Australian accent. "No, not manager. I have had to work many hours though."

A small loud plane flies over them making its course.

Jagger can barely make out what they are saying with the plane noise. He doesn't want to move and cannot believe how close Garth and the man is in proximity of him. It's the first time he has been near him for longer than sixty-seconds.

The plane finishes its intrusion and Jagger is able to make out a little of their words.

Garth is getting his pilot license for fun. He works off of some kind of computer fighter flight training program thing.

Jagger moves around onto the sand and stands his board against the railing. He is going to enjoy this moment. He loves how attentive, strong and yet delicate Garth is with the older man. It's like he wants to listen to him and cares. Why can't more be like him? He watches the way he stands examining every part of his body, like the tattoo wrapped around his bicep like barbed wire. His green eyes turning hazel when the wind and sun hit them at just the right angle.

Jagger diverts his attention anywhere else so that he doesn't appear to be too into him. His heart pounds nervously in a panic that Garth can hear it. Garth suddenly adjusts his standing position to be able to watch Jagger too. They both do everything they can to not move from their comfortable spots for twenty minutes with no one else around, but the oblivious older man.

Garth likes to walk around with change in his pockets sometimes. If there's no change in there, he puts his hands in his pockets. He likes to read the paper and walk around with it, holding it under his arm like an old soul.

He wears a barely noticeable thin gold bracelet on his left wrist. The left side of his mouth opens wider than his right when he smiles. Sometimes he walks fast with intention and speed to his destination as if he's late to a fire bell. Other times he strolls with his hands in his pockets as if what's missing is Jagger on his arm, a park with trees all around, stars in the sky and a soundtrack playing. Either his grandparents raised him or a pack of wolves.

Jagger picks up his surfboard and takes a walk across the sand until he reaches the ocean. He moves into the water and lays the board down. Lying on his stomach on top of the surfboard, he paddles out to sea allowing the breaking waves to splash over him in a baptism. When he reaches his comfortable distance at sea, he turns to face the shore. A wave forms and he immediately grabs the sides of his board and pops up on top of it. He bends his knees and leans forward allowing the wave to carry him as he carves out on the wave. Garth smiles in the distance watching him and listening to the old man at the same time.

The remains of the heat saturate the beaches of Southern California while the boys hang around at Russell's house with drinks in plastic cups. Slade and Russell converse privately behind the sliding glass door of the living room that peers out at the pool.

"He's been so down lately." Slade tells Russell watching Jagger outside.

"He seems okay now." Russell says, "He looks rather good actually." Russell opens the sliding door and heads out back.

Jagger sits up from one of the chairs in the backyard and walks around the pool. "When are people coming?"

"About now." Russell promises.

Slade walks out into the backyard shirtless flaunting his body as usual heading towards Jagger.

Jagger says, "They always show up when we've become anti-social or..."

"Blacked out." Slade interrupts wrapping an arm tightly around Jagger in a friendly pat.

Russell cranks up the huge grill near the pool. "They'll be here."

Russell eyes Jagger pacing around barefoot and his jeans perfectly fit on his tight body accentuating his ass. "Did you get new jeans?"

"These? No. I just don't wear them that often or I wear them when I don't have shoes on. They look better that way."

"They look better off." Slade says typically.

Russell smiles seeing how intoxicating Jagger looks and how that's making him feel. "You were a skater boy at one point and failed to mention it."

Russell cranks up the grill and tosses various meats and chickens on it. Slade grabs some sunscreen lotion on one of the patio tables.

"Hey Slade. How did it go with that guy last night?" Russell asks, "What was it bachelor number one thousand and forty-seven?"

Slade hands Jagger the lotion gesturing for him to put it on him. Jagger takes it and faces Slade with it. Slade closes his eyes waiting. "After he sucked me off I thought I would return the favor. I sucked his cock and then he came in my mouth without telling me."

Jagger tries to open the bottle to squeeze the lotion out with no luck.

"Oh shit." Russell says.

Troy heads over to Jagger and Slade filming with his little flip camera.

"So I spit it back on him." Slade explains.

"Give a dude warning. Not everybody likes it." Jagger says.

"I would've at least wanted the warning." Slade says.

The lotion suddenly squirts out a lot from the bottle like cum hitting Slade in the face and chest. Jagger and Slade start laughing. Slade wipes it off handing the remains to Jagger.

Jagger notices Troy filming with his camera irritated. "Troy, what are you doing?"

"Oh, I didn't realize this was a private moment between you two." Troy says.

Slade smirks bringing his pinky to the corner of his lip and using a goofy voice. "Not anymorrrre." He laughs and walks away yanking his shorts up a little.

"I'm through with boys." Troy tells Jagger.

"I'm through with love." Jagger replies.

Russell's eyes narrow not buying it.

Jagger notices this. "What?"

Slade chimes in, "That's because every dude you touch gets pregnant."

"Hey!" Jagger shouts jokingly.

Slade moves into a run, forms a cannon ball and jumps into the pool.

One by one people start arriving at the party. Jagger jogs through the house to open the front door. The music blares around him through the sound system in the house.

Jagger works the crowd and overhears a woman in her early 40's vent about a guy she was dating and having problems with. He intercepts the conversation. "How long were you seeing each other?"

She stands in her tight cocktail dress, one pigtail above the side of her head. She sips nervously from her drink. "About a year and a half." Her smile is plastered, but warm and genuine nonetheless. "We fought over his constant cigarette smoking and how he's non-communicative in every way."

"After you guys fought did you call him?" Jagger tends to be overly inquisitive with others and their relationship issues. It helps him study love and write about it.

"The next day I did." She said.

"Has he called you back?" Jagger asks.

"No."

"How long ago was this?"

"A month ago."

"And no word?" Jagger questions.

"Right." She smiles.

"You tried once and..."

"Well, I tried one more time a week later. I left a message and said something like, *What the hell is going on?*"

Jagger says, "Hmm let me guess, nothing after that one."

"Pretty much, but I was over it. Once I came home and he was there. I purposely didn't say anything to see how long it would take for him to say a word."

"Oh yeah, how long?" Jagger asks.

"After twenty minutes I couldn't take it anymore and finally said, 'How was your day?'"

"Wow." Jagger shakes his head chuckling and wanders away. He sits down next to Troy at one of the patio tables near the entry to the back of the house. Troy is very buzzed. He is talking to some guy named Barrett.

"Jagger!" Troy realizes Jagger is sitting next to him. He throws his arms around Jagger's neck tightly and says to Barrett, "I love this dude!"

"Okay, love you too." Realizing how drunk he is, Jagger tries to remove the weight of Troy's hands from around him.

Troy says to Barrett, "This guy taught me to be responsible in a relationship." He tells Jagger, "You're the only one that's taught me to be a MAN!"

"Someone had to do it." Jagger mumbles.

Troy laughs and continues talking to Barrett

Jagger notices someone new sitting on the other side of him at the table. It's Jacob, this nineteen-year-old friend of Troy's.

Jacob opens up with Jagger immediately about his story about this 26-year-old guy he went on a date with named Steven. Jacob said the guy and the date were perfect. "I liked him and we didn't have sex."

"Nice." Jagger said, "Romantic."

Steven told Jacob that he wanted to see him again and said, "Let's see each other next Monday." It turns out Steven was doing some camping thing with his parents that day though.

Jacob called him and there was no answer, then like the little deviant we become when are being ignored, he blocked his number hours later and tried calling again. That's what some do when they don't get a response the second time around. Others call it playing games, but in this case they're both partaking in the game playing.

Jacob called Steven while his number was blocked and the guy answered this time.

"Hello, what's up?" Jacob said to him.

"Hello?" The guy asked twice as if there were a bad connection - which there wasn't.

"What's up?" Jacob asked.

"I'm camping today with my parents." Steven said.

"Will we get to see each other tonight?"

"Um, I'm going to go with, no." Steven says aloof.

"I understand if you don't want to see me."

"No, it's not that. I'm busy here, but if you say things like that it makes me not want to see you."

Jacob wonders why he had to say that.

Jagger says, "Eww. He's a jerk.", but then again maybe Jacob might've been too presumptuous. Steven should have had some dignity to let Jacob know that it wasn't going to happen. They are both to blame in this scenario. Steven led him on and wasn't honest, while Jacob was more into him than Steven was. It's a recipe for a disaster.

Jagger looks over at the big screen in the house playing an Eagles concert. The shot seems a little grainy to him. He responds to Jacob about Steven. "He sounds like an ass."

"He is an ass. What about you?" Jacob asks.

"Me? I've had the shit summer of dating. I was picking the wrong dudes, by a lot!"

"Who is the fucker?"

"Fuckers. Plural. I've been busy. There's been more than one. It's been an interesting few months, but I got my revenge I guess you could say. I fucked up Caden's board. Piper got his tires slashed while my friend urinated on his front door. Nevada got a drink thrown in his face."

"Whoa! Cool!"

"Oh God no. Not cool. I guess I got a little out of control. I have a little temper."

"Damn, I would love to do all of that to some people. You're so strong and brave!"

"No. It wasn't the best way for me to handle it. I should've walked away, but I'm not good with that. I'm working on that trait. Walking away is strong. Fighting is weak. It's letting your ego get a hold of you."

Troy stands up exuberant, drunk and loud. "Wait a minute I'll be right back!" He turns around to head into the house, but instead walks right into the screen door falling on top of it. The screen bends inward inside the house onto the floor. Troy lands on it crushing it. Half his body is inside the house. The other half is outside. He is on all fours. Russell runs over. Jagger looks over a little buzzed with his mouth open not knowing what just happened.

"Oh wow!" Barrett jumps up and grabs Troy to help him up.

"No, I have it! I have it okay!" Troy shouts.

Jagger busts out laughing extremely loud.

Troy comes to and attempts to stand up.

Jagger can't contain himself. "I thought the concert playing on the T.V. seemed a little grainy! The screen was closed that's why!"

Russell chuckles and helps Troy up. "It was a bad screen. I've been meaning to get it replaced."

"Troy!" Jagger calls to him, "Come here and sit down. Tell me what you need and I'll go get it okay. I can't bear you wandering around like that getting into mischief."

Troy rises up slow, slightly delirious and unsure of what happened.

CHAPTER 15

Jagger's Revolution

Jagger walks into Russell's living room from the back sliding door only to find Troy and Slade arguing.

"Dude, you don't know what you're taking. This is bad shit." Slade says.

"You don't know anything about it. Mind your own business!"

Jagger approaches them. "Guys. What's going on?"

"Troy's up to his hypochondriac shit again." Slade says.

"He doesn't know what he's talking about." Troy tells Jagger.

"You should get a load of the shit he's taking. Look at this stuff." Slade grabs the bottles of the various pills on the counter

Jagger reads the bottles shocked. "This is for blood sugar levels." He looks at Troy perplexed and worried. "Your blood sugar isn't low."

"You don't know that. How come I'm always tired?" Troy is always finding something wrong with him and reading up on stuff, then dreaming up Cancer. He's part of the youth culture obsessed with outer looks.

"There could be many explanations for that. You're self-diagnosing yourself and you can't do that. You're fine. You're perfect." Jagger explains to him.

"Nope, this stuff is good for you. Trust me I checked on it." Troy is insistent.

Slade walks away and plops on the couch. He sits back and puts his hand on his forehead sliding his fingers through his hair.

Jagger reads one of the other bottles. "It's fine for you to want be healthy and take care of yourself. You already do that. You work out religiously. You eat healthy. You know your fucking hot, but don't go looking for problems that you don't have. You know what you need to do? You need to stop thinking and be happy. No one is getting off this planet alive. At least no one I know. So don't go looking for trouble you don't need."

Troy nods. "I know but you don't understand, I've read about this and it's the latest best thing for your body. I know there are going to be risks with anything you take. You don't need to tell me that."

Slade adds, "Yeah and where are you getting this information from? The fashion, entertainment and gossip magazines? MTV?"

Jagger interjects, "And pop culture and what singer is doing what. I know. We've become so focused on our senses and celebrities and with what gives us pleasure."

Russell comes out of the bedroom and heads into the kitchen that is open to the living room.

This is deeper to Jagger than the pills. He's watched this world blow up and become infatuated over triviality. They fixate over bullshit in other people's lives obsessing about who's fucking who over and who's in porn.

Jagger goes on a major rant, "We've got people living in Ethiopia or Uganda and they don't give a damn about what they look like or if they feel validated. They're trying to feed their kids. I'm sorry I hate to see that. People in other cultures don't have the opportunity to act like us. People don't have the opportunity to do that in fucking New Orleans right now. Who cares what you look like! We live in this bubble of a world and frankly I'm sick of it. All we give a shit about is our ripped abs and our Botox and who's hot. We're so shallow. And I know I've been guilty of it too. We look at the rest of the world in such a limited point of view, but the biggest fucking drag is the self-focus. The focus of it's all about me and let me examine myself." He makes a mock annoyed voice of the people he's describing, "...and how do I feel, am I validated, am I okay in the world." He slams back as Jagger, "Give me a break, you know, go build a house for homeless people in Zimbabwe or something. People are selfish, spoiled, obnoxious, uncaring human beings."

Everyone is quiet. Slade sits back and looks out the big window to the backyard thinking about what he's saying. Troy stares at the floor knowing it's true. Russell stops what he is doing and watches from the kitchen mesmerized by Jagger's speech.

Jagger delves intensely deep, "We did start as the greatest country ever," He nods with half a mock smirk, "We came here. We struggled. We suffered. We made colonies. We made it to be a certain way. We fought like everybody else. We fought to the death for our freedom. We had a revolution and became a free society. We broke the chains that bound us and the declaration of independence was written. We were all considered equal. We had honor. We were good people. Are we not supposed to look at the homeless guy down the street? We're like animals! We're not human. Actually, we're not any different than animals. Oh wait, except we have intelligence and free will." He pauses burnt out for a beat,

"Everyone is self-consumed. Self-consumed with their bodies. Consumed with their psyches. Go volunteer for a charity somewhere and then I'll be impressed. We're so fucking media focused and lost and.... "

Troy's cell phone rings breaking Jagger's point. Everyone is quiet and Jagger gestures for him to answer it. Troy grabs his phone and wanders away. Jagger sits on the couch next to Slade letting out a sigh. Slade's arm reaches around him tenderly. Jagger's head falls against Slade's body defeated. Slade brings him in closer looking out for his friend who can be passionate and moving, but wears himself out and has to retreat. Jagger shuts his eyes. Slade plops his feet on the coffee table. He crashes and closes his eyes too.

Troy hangs up the phone and sits on the couch next to them lying back against Jagger.

All three doze off worn out from it all.

Russell sticks bottles of beer into a bucket of ice. He walks past the boys lounging and opens the sliding door to the backyard. He sets it down and gets his grill on turning the music on in the back.

They are each other's right hand. They all know they will have each other's back and be there no matter what. They are their own tight unit. They are not out, they are in. They are their own family unit of love and with their own home base of possibilities. They grow strong as time moves on. The future shows more greatness in their wake. They have their own utopia and their own renegade, one of true empathy for all. They see all the differences and all the colors that inhabit each individual. They are all separate entities linked to one purpose, one definition, one destination of all light and reception.

There's something to say about those that never cross the line with one another and maintain a friendship without benefits. There is too much respect to let emotions or the physical get in the way of this utopian brother renegade the four boys have created. They have formed an alliance in search of promoting truth in this warped culture.

It's sometimes a difficult thing for two guys who are into guys to be friends or sociable without wanting to get in their pants. You can't talk to them about someone you met that you're into. They get jealous or upset and have to go. They don't want to talk about it and that's not a friend. The boys have found something for life. It's a life sentence that they want to be in because they can have that with each other and not run into repressing themselves or worry about someone's intention to bed them or put a ring on their finger. Their friendship is not premeditated, but is genuine and real. They know the truth. They don't need to hear it. It's a symbiotic hand gesture. Holding up a peace sign, bringing your hand to your heart and then simulating a joint inhale followed by a cough.

Friends are like that of a sports team. Sports teams have some of the best positive human qualities that carry over to your personal and business life. You have groups solidified by cooperating with each other. To succeed they have complete communication. The group is able to then work through conflicts and come to a resolution.

How is it two straight guys can have a lifelong friendship and for two gay guys it's rare or nearly impossible? There are too many sexual undertones, urges and attractions going on. It's mostly acted on at some point. If it doesn't happen, it's because only one of the guys is attracted to their friend more than the other is. Some won't bother to be your friend or talk to you if you don't look and act a certain way that jives with their superficial perception. No effort is made into looking deeper into the soul of who this guy is who desires a friendship. Maybe it's because there isn't any of that touchiness with straight guys. You don't have to watch what you say, whereas with the latter, you do. The latter being like some of today's American women. Chunky bitches who are 5 foot 5, 180 pounds with short hair and a negative attitude. When a straight guy is friends with another guy it is not based on the guy's looks in the slightest. It's based on mutual interests and conversational styles. They are the least shallow of friendships that are formed. Fraternities are another camaraderie group minus some of the violent controversies. Fraternities are a group that defines brotherhood where they push for strong bonds. If done positively their goal is to encourage camaraderie. Their goal together is one of bonding. Brothers are all one when they agree. They can alter an entire planet in a positive way when they work together.

CHAPTER 16

Cupid's Arrow

An oasis in the sun casts a rich spell of color across the sky. The Summer season is coming to an end and it's time for the huge annual Hermosa Beach Surfing Summer festival party. This is surf city and the weather couldn't be more perfect on this hottest day of the year on record. The temperature rises in the air and elevates hormones in the process. Hot tanned girls in bikinis walk around with stiff drinks while boys in shorts walk around with stiff woody's. Some hold surfboards like an accessory, while others hold cold beer. Rock music plays loud and blares outwardly from all angles. Hot bodies grind each other to the music. There's the smell of barbecue in the air. The sun beats down hard like the burning edges of a fire. Pulsating sounds smash against the bodies in sensual richness. The party is filled with astounding carved out men and stunning women. It's a smaller scale to South Beach. Those that work out hard and play harder are evident in the crowd. Beer trucks pull up in the distance to promote their products. Water sports of every variety are carried on by the enviably tanned and fit on boards in the ocean.

Jagger has grown more into himself over the past number of months. He's completely content and happy with the slight twinges of melancholy that creep in for a slight peek. The roar of the joyful crowd on the sands glide on the wind that has picked up suddenly. It blows the scent of BBQ around. Jagger takes in a deep breath in and closes his eyes moving his face into the strong, heated wind feeling salvation and redemption. The warmth of the wind bends the swaying palm trees.

Jagger, Slade, Troy and Russell sit around camped out at the best table at the top of the stairs that overlooks the massive crowd. They throw back some of that good old-fashioned boy conversation. They talk over each other like a Woody Allen movie.

Jagger daydreams feeling bliss as the boys talk over each other. He comes to and stands up impatient, slamming his hands on the table. "I'm going for a walk. Maybe I'll be back. Maybe I won't."

Jagger walks away from the gang and stands at the top of the stairs watching the mob scene below. He strolls slowly along the railing watching the swarms of people having a good time. The music is loud and pounding against the surf. The pavement is packed with people. Half of them dance to the music while the other half drink and bellow loud.

One foot at a time he places his hand on the rail moving in hesitation towards the crowd. He sports a dark blue T-shirt, board shorts and flip-flops. He looks better looking than ever before. Maybe it's the sun hitting him at the right angle or maybe it's his newfound self. His looks get increasingly defined, attractive and more enhanced when he's not hidden in clothes. You can see his skin and the shape of his body, which is visibly toned up close.

A blonde girl in a bikini makes out with a bleached blonde surfer boy and falls on him. Girls laugh having a good time as they pass him. Boys are huddled with boys, girls are with girls. Hot shiny racing cars pull up and park close.

It all suddenly quiets around him as his mind wanders. He glances up towards the northern sky and hears *them*. The angels and Spirit have cracked open through the portal to him. He can hear the other side clearly. The sun casts purple, orange, yellow and red color rays like finger paint across a canvas on the sky. Jagger's smile grows feeling good and triumphant. He is militant, a soldier and a warrior of love. He's close to the angels for the first time in a long time. He can hear their voices. *Open your eyes. Open your eyes.* The words are repeating and overlapping itself in his left ear. A tough wind picks up incredibly strong and blows through him. People chase after paper plates and napkins that go flying in the air. Jagger takes another step down on the stairs that leads to the crowd below. His smile is cocky and sexy in place. His eyes open back up to the vast sky finding peace as he takes another deep breath in and exhales.

He extends his gaze towards the biblical bright yellow and purple shaded sky. A red rose petal blows sloppily in the wind and stalls in front of him on an invisible platform for seconds. He reaches out latching onto it. He looks at it and then around to see where it's coming from. He sees a few more petals blowing in the wind over the crowd. The petals are every shade: Red, pink, white and orange. The petals are being shot out of a machine in the parking lot like confetti.

The aroma in the air is a drug that is filled with sugar. It is absinthe, wine and roses. There is heat in the air caused by the flamed torches and mini bonfires scattered around the parking lot that's converted into the party next to the sand.

He watches the crowd disburse clearing the section in front of him as he continues down the stairs slowly. The crowd splits as if it's a wedding and he's walking down the aisle to his groom. He strolls down the path to his mate. His entourage is back at the top of the stairs goofing off and being rowdy. They appear in slow motion to him as he's made his way to the bottom of the steps. He holds onto the petal, gloriously alone, solo, and much more approachable. His curves and newly formed muscles in his back take shape through his shirt as he stretches grabbing another petal. He focuses on a group of girls in string bikini swimwear laughing together. He notices one is on skates. They head towards one of the bars set up on the side of the parking lot. A group of shirtless guys shake and pour water on each other being disruptive. It's maddening chaos and he loves it.

It puzzles him why it never works out with any of these former guys. He thought it was them and then he thought it was himself. He's learned that it was not going anywhere or happening because it's not supposed to. His path was set a long time ago with someone else. It's been decided who he's supposed to go on the trip with. You can't fuck with that or fate.

A hot shiny purple rod car skids off making a loud screeching echo. The crowd in the center aisle systematically takes a step away from each other again as if peeling the layers of a flower to reveal Garth in all his glory. Garth stands in place against a wall directly across from Jagger. He's got his red lifeguard shorts on and a white T-shirt on. His hands are in his pockets, very cool with eyes as pure as a quartz crystal. He's been waiting there all his life with a look that's been in place for some time. He's been watching Jagger. The look is directed right onto him as if he knew he would be standing there on the steps waiting for him. He is his groom.

Jagger glances up and locks eyes with him with surprise. His eyes open and this time he does not let go of him. He thought Garth was gone for good. He had given up, but all of that good stuff is rushing back into him. The heavens are not closed after all. Hopes and private wishes are responded to and love will come home even beyond endless past lives from before.

It's incredibly noble when a guy becomes an adult by taking responsibility with what he knows he wants. He buckles up and makes a move to make it happen. It's your job to reciprocate that and reward him for his bravery because at that moment he's earned it. If you don't respond or give anything back, then your appeal is lower than the magnified dignity he displays.

Jagger's eyes open wide letting all the light in that Garth is projecting on him. You never realize the road you've traveled until you stop to look behind you. They both see the trail behind them blazed with fire, lighting the aisle to be bound for good. Jagger forgets about all the others and knows an honest guy is in front of him. His heart races with nerves unable to move.

A slight smile and nod appears and grows on Garth's face as they swim in each other's ocean. Jagger remains cautious and unsure of what to do or where to go. He heads towards him a little bit in the open pathway. He panics underneath looking around him.

Garth moves away from the wall with his hands comfortably in his pockets as he strolls towards Jagger. The saying that time literally stops when the magic happens is true. Jagger is filled with nerves trembling like the leaves on the palm trees surrounding them. His mouth opens trying to breath in as much oxygen to keep from falling over. He has a level of intensity and honesty that few can match that can overwhelm many. There are a few that are strong enough to take it. The one that can is the one for you.

Garth walks through the partygoers like a floating angel, moving closer to Jagger focused only on him. Jagger attempts to dodge another way, but no one is going to let that happen.

Jagger hears a voice directed at him.

"Hey." Garth sounds scratchy like the sexy morning voice one would have who hasn't used their vocal cords in a while, but this is how he typically sounds.

Jagger stops unable to move. Garth is right there standing there not moving and speaking to him. He can't get away. His breath stalls and grabs him lifting him up into another plane as if he were a spirit crossing over. Jagger stands with strong sexy confidence, but inside he shakes like the San Andreas Fault cracking open wide. He is face to face with Garth who is bold like good wine, like Jagger had been his all along.

"Hi." Jagger's voice is full of grit and seduction. He is in top form and knows this is it. He is stunned that Garth is standing inches from him and actually striking up a conversation.

They study every inch of their faces as they navigate nervously through their almost wordless conversation. This is the closest they had ever been to each other physically. The crowd evaporates off the pavement and allows them room. Make a quick decision on how far you want to become involved when you're presented with goodness.

Their breathing sounds loud to themselves, but is silent to the other one no matter how hard they attempt to control it.

Garth looks down at the pavement bashfully then back at Jagger. "How's it goin' mate?"

Jagger fixates at the people around them in silence. He is aware they are present, but they fade out of him. His entire body beats like a native drum on some forgotten tropical island in the middle of the Pacific. He shudders and floats in the air as if on ecstasy. "Good." A thin inviting smile creeps up on his face. It gives Garth the sunshine he's looking for.

A smile appears on Garth satisfied. He nods nervously. "So, you're Jagger?"

"Yeah, you know who I am?" Jagger is stunned and taken aback. The sexual tension is overflowing in both of their cups.

"Yeah, mate." Garth rips another smile across his face nodding. "I'm Garth."

Jagger wants to say he knows, but instead plays it off. "Nice to meet you." His hand moves through the air towards him to shake his. Jagger memorizes the shape of his hand as Garth's hand falls into his.

"Bang on." Garth chuckles.

Jagger's mind races all over the place wanting to fall over, but he is being held up by Garth's cables.

"Nice to meet you Jagger." His smile opens wide from ear to ear. His pierced dimples display like jagged edges.

They clasp eyes without evading and unsure of where to go next or what to say next. They have their full attention and don't want the other one to cut this conversation short and leave prematurely. *Don't blow it. Don't be afraid.*

"Uh," Garth stumbles on his words, "I've seen you before and I thought you might be here today." He wants to say I hoped you would be here.

"You did?" Jagger can't believe it. He feels as if he is dreaming or in some bizarre drug induced trance.

"Yeah, is that cool or scary as shit man?" Garth laughs.

"Yeah," Jagger nods in shock attempting to grow nerves of steel. "No, I mean, yeah of course it's cool, not scary at all."

Garth keeps smiling. "Awesome."

They look at each other anxious with the occasional nervous smile coming on. They want to stay in front of the other forever, but they know they're going to have to try to have a conversation no matter how hard the butterflies take over.

Garth is in a panic of what to say. "What are you up to?"

Jagger looks around for his circle, his brothers, and comrades in life, "I'm supposed to go to a bbq, but..." He looks up at his friends playing in the distance then back at him, "....but I'm not sure if I'm going to go." Jagger implies hoping Garth picks up on it.

Garth nods and looks to see what Jagger is looking at or if he can see his friends and know more.

Garth asks, "Would you maybe be interested or like to go out sometime or now perhaps?" He laughs off his embarrassment and feelings of intimidation. It's hard enough asking someone of the opposite sex out, but the risk for embarrassment or humiliation is higher with someone of the same sex. The guy who is up for the challenge is noteworthy of some very important elements of bravery that others don't have.

Jagger laughs a little at his sudden coyness and wants him to feel at ease. "Yeah. I would love too. Now would be great."

Garth's whole body smiles and he allows his soul to be captured. "Good." Garth smiles and wants to wrap his love around Jagger.

They stroll through the crowd moving closer to each other with the continuous shy glances in awe.

Slade notices their exchange from afar and taps Russell. "Hey guys, guys....look." He points down to Jagger and Garth who are smiling, chuckling and feeling comfortable talking to one another.

Russell says, "Well, I'll be damned."

Troy laughs, "Yes! He's in. He's got him. He's got him."

Garth and Jagger stroll through the crowd moving comfortably close to each other as if they've been together for years. They steal coy eye contact with one another in the process. Garth has his hands comfortably in his pockets cool and content walking next to Jagger.

Jagger notices the boys at the top of the staircase. Slade, Russell and Troy have their mouths open in awe with radiant smiles. Jagger shrugs at them, gesturing towards Garth without him noticing. He mouths the words in their direction, '*This is the guy.*'

Russell smiles grabbing Slade and patting him playfully on the head. Slade's eyes are full of magic. Troy nods with a smile and gives him the thumbs up.

CHAPTER 17

Jagger and Garth: The Date.

At a popular classy restaurant in Hermosa Beach lit up to perfection, Jagger and Garth approach the stairwell. They find a table that miraculously appears to be set up for them on the outside patio. The patio part of the restaurant is made of wood and the pillars are built into the sand with a view of the sunset over the ocean. The tall gas light posts click on. The white lights strung over the patio turn on as well. They both sit down together at an out of the way table.

"Wow." Jagger says, "So, uh," pointing to Garth, "that accent is uh-Australian?"

"Yeah mate." Garth is lively and excessively excited that Jagger is sitting across from him.

Jagger nods afraid to speak. "I'm intrigued, what part of the country?"

"Brisbane. Been out here for about a year and a half, probably explains a lot. I've only been in the gay world for about two years so I'm not experienced in it all that much."

"You seem to be good with me."

"That's because I can't stop watching you. You're a good looking guy, but I've sensed more than that in you. I can't explain it."

"You've only been in the gay world for two years? What happened before that? You were with women?" Jagger asks.

"Yeah realized women weren't for me and had brushed off any gay idea before that. Although I love women, but I'm into guys too if it's the right one."

Jagger wants to know every little detail and flaw about Garth and to caress it and hold it to him tight. "Oh yeah? Tell me more about you and don't leave anything out. I'm a bit of a journalist so forgive my questions, but I've been curious about you too."

Garth laughs, "Well okay, I've been out here nearly two years and I love it. That's when I decided to make a drastic change. I miss my friends back home sometimes. We'd have a whistle and a bit of a giggle when we'd go out."

While living in Australia, Garth used to play in a Rugby League during the winter and then in the summer he would be a volunteer Life Saver. He loved helping people and being close to the water. When he moved to Southern California it was easy to get work as a lifeguard with that experience. He had most of the training and skills already. He loves being outdoors too so it was the perfect gig not to mention as he says, "As well as indoor activities in the bedroom." He adds making implications with Jagger. "I loved dancing at the clubs, but also spending the night alone with someone special, dinner, strolling along the beach, pashing and making out. This."

Garth is annoyed that most guys want to get into his jeans. He's been looking to meet a guy that has more on his mind than sex. He wants to form a friendship first and if that works out then a genuine lifetime relationship. He believes all relationships must be a 50/50 basis to work properly and wants to settle down to a full time relationship eventually. His eye has been on Jagger since he first saw him. He's equally as sexual as him, but also wants love, commitment and a relationship. He can get all that and more from him and knows this from reading Jagger's column. He hasn't done a lot before in the way of sex. He loves kissing, hugging, jacking off, sucking, and especially loves 69. He's never done anal or as he boldly states, "Still a virgin ass. I have been saving that for when I meet the right guy." Garth's smile lights the path for Jagger.

What he has to say is right on the money with him. He's similar to Jagger in many ways. He wants to know someone on a friendship level and allow things to develop easily over time. Garth is very loyal in friendship and in intimate relationships.

"It's all or nothing with me too." Jagger contributes.

"Man," Garth says, "It's cool to meet someone who has the same ideas as yourself, especially someone as good looking as you." Garth is a little flirt with him, but he's been waiting for this moment for some time and doesn't want to underplay or blow it. He doesn't play games and with the Aussie nature comes being bold and direct.

Jagger gets a little flustered and out of his league. He looks away trying to hide, then back at Garth while listening to him open up as if he hadn't been able to confide openly with anyone.

"I hope that I'll get the chance to get to know you better, although I guess someone like you has many guys interested in you." Garth doesn't want to flatter him as he means it, but there is a trace of wanting to know more. He wants to make sure he isn't going after someone who has guys lined up to date him. As long as Jagger is a one man guy and not swayed or bored easily with what he's got, then he's found his man.

"No, it's you who probably has them clawing at your door." Jagger tells him.

Garth smiles, "I don't open the door for them. I'd love to get to know you and for you to know me. Get to become friends and then see if it leads anywhere. It would be ace to be friends with you."

Jagger is quiet and thinking, *um- friends*?

"What do you think man?" Garth asks.

"A friend? Yeah, that would be nice to be friends." Jagger is afraid to leap. He had been through the ringer often with a guy and for nothing. It's not uncommon to tiptoe gently around another one, but Garth is different. This is his crush! He's been waiting for this his whole life.

Garth is hardhearted, yet sensitive and has a great capacity for love with the right person. He's as hesitant as Jagger is about giving his heart away for fear of it being broken. He is too trusting as he takes people at their word.

Jagger nods, "I don't bounce from relationship to relationship by choice." He is the consummate Don Juan. "I can't because once I choose someone I'm there for better or worse. That's the person that I choose to be with to go the distance with. I've filtered through many disastrous dates that lead absolutely nowhere. I've given up on that. Although many other opportunities presented itself to me, I've recently chosen to stay single until I find him." Then he confesses, "I don't know if I've been in real love now that I think about it, but I've had a little crush on you for some time I should probably admit that now."

"A little crush on me have yah?" Garth's face lights up like Time Square ready to make more moves and let himself in with Jagger. "Never been in love with a guy, but sure as hell could do so with a guy like you. I've been watching you since I first saw you. I thought you'd never talk to a guy like me. Believe in the old saying that the eyes are the windows to the soul. When I see you, I see beautiful eyes, a handsome face and now I can definitely say a warm, caring and loving nature. I had hoped one day to meet the guy destined for me and felt that if it didn't happen I would never settle for second best. I don't play the field as I don't believe in casual sex at all."

Jagger is uncomfortable and doesn't want to tell him of all the bad sex flings he's had. He'd be tossed aside for good.

Garth continues, "I want a man who is a man, yet sensitive enough to have romance with. I want to love and be loved. I know that sounds cliché, but I don't care. If I can't have a special guy to share my love, then I will stay single for if it happens it has to be forever. I get hurt easily even though I have a tough exterior, but once the shell is cracked, I am vulnerable. There you have my complicated personality."

"Are you complicated?" Jagger asks. "We're all compartments of complication I guess though. You've widened my eyes more and you're blowing me away. I appreciate you being so candid immediately. You have a charismatic way with words. I'm a big talker and when I'm not doing that I'm writing it all down, but now I'm speechless."

Two hours have passed and they've grown immediately comfortable with each other laughing and bonding over verbal tennis. It is as if they have been brothers through dozens of lifetimes. Jagger wonders, *"How could wanting this with this guy for this long feel torturous? Now that it's happening it's as natural as can be."* They were guided to one another for a reason. Their souls split right down the middle at conception. It is impossible for them to not have made contact as it's been contracted and destined long before they came to be.

They both leave the restaurant and head down to the beach playing like raucous boys, jumping over the stair rails seizing each other in heated and playful ways.

"Hey." Garth grabs him and grows suddenly quiet facing Jagger.

Garth hangs onto him with both his hands. "Man you melt me like butter with a hot knife. I wish I could look at you without getting goose bumps on my spine, a head spin in my brain and a stiffie in my cock." Garth is blown into intimidating nerves by the force of Jagger's eyes. "Damn, your eyes show me more than you can say." He moves in close towards Jagger flirting with him. "I see honesty, love, compassion and trust from you." He backs away boastful, "But my dick sees another interpretation. For it has a mind of its own and refuses to stay down." He jumps back and leaps like a wild kid back over the stairwell.

Jagger laughs in love, "You're nuts!"

Garth jumps back down happy in front of Jagger. "Man, you are making me the luckiest guy in the whole world. I have to stop my heart from thumping in my chest. I like you a lot mate."

"I like you too boy. Damnit." Jagger shakes his head not believing this is happening.

They find a place to sit down on a closed lifeguard tower with no one around. Garth recently arrived in L.A. from a visit back home in Brisbane, Australia. He had been there for a few weeks and told Jagger all about the trip. He had also recently started waiting tables a couple of nights a week to save a few more bucks at the "Beached Hut." He said his main goal is to eventually become a Fireman.

Winters in Australia are in their high seventies and in the Spring it cools down to about the high sixties. The spring brings their usual normal changes where the grass starts to green up and the trees start to blossom. The winter had been a record dry one and the whole state ended up in the middle of a drought. To top it off, there had been another "El-Nino" forecast so the Aussie summer rain fell as well. Los Angeles isn't blessed with the changing of the leaves when Fall comes. It gets cooler, crispier and a little windy to tell everyone that Fall is here and Winter is on its way.

It took Garth back to recent days. He remembered that at the start of spring signaled his final season playing Rugby before he came out to L.A. He had too many spinal injuries in the games and couldn't afford any more. "My spine had taken enough knocks before I got out here that I should've known when to quit."

Jagger leans closer to Garth and puts his hand on his shoulder like they have been together for years. Garth leans in more and lifts his arm up and puts it around Jagger tightly pulling him against his side, both hearts pounding hard being so close.

"So you had a wipe out?" Jagger asks.

"Yeah, well one good thing though, the Rugby clobbering didn't affect my participation in Surf Life Saving. Actually swimming has helped to strengthen it. The only thing I had to consider giving up was the surfboat trials, but that was about it. It was scary as shit man."

Garth was grateful to get to go back home for a while. He found that socially life was even better than when he was there last. This could be because he had time away from it. You miss things more when you don't see them for a while and therefore have more appreciation for it. When he was there last, the city had the seafood festival, then there was the State Fair (called the Ekka). On one of the other weekends was the "River of Fire." Garth animatedly describes it with his hands over the ocean.

"The whole mid-city area of the River was a mass of fireworks. It was one of the biggest we had." Garth explains, "The highlight of the evening was the fly over of the Flll's with their after burners spewing flames. It could be seen for miles." His face glows as he loses himself like a kid at a carnival. "Aw mate it was bloody ace watching it. I went to a barby afterwards and the weekend after that was the Strawberry Festival. I hadn't danced my ass at the parties for ages. I had to stick to the straight clubs though as I am sick of drama at the gay clubs. I wish you were there with me." He checks out Jagger in admiration. "You could be my main bloke on my arm."

"I would be. I wish I had been there too, maybe next time we'll go together. I can understand you not frequenting gay clubs as many have run into unwanted dramatic trouble. I almost never go unless one of my friends insists or demands it. I've become bored with the ambiance in the end anyway." He says to Garth, "You are a true poet with an amazing heart, a good guy to the end I bet."

Garth is dead on to him. "Sweet mate! You sure know how to make someone feel special." He daydreams focusing out over the ocean, "Not sure anyone has ever done that for me before...." He looks back at Jagger, "....make me feel like I am the most important person. It's me not you that is the luckiest guy in the world. You make me feel there is no one else in the whole world sitting next to you for the last what it is four hours now?" He chuckles at how fast the time has flown by while with him.

They gaze at each other nervously, then Garth leans in slow to kiss Jagger. Both of their whole bodies light up on fire feeling the kiss everywhere. Garth's lips are soft, yet strong. He tries to hold back and not go in for the kill in an intense hot kiss. He wants to keep the first one light and polite, no tongue. Jagger tries hard to think of something else, because every time he looks at Garth his cock grows. He is not trying to sexualize him, but his kiss hits him everywhere. They pull back and stare at each other smiling, then back out at the ocean. A star breaks across the sky bursting into many pieces dripping like scratch marks on a wall.

Jagger moves up to the lifeguard railing. "Whoa shit did you see that?"

Garth gets up and puts his arm around Jagger, then leans his body into him with affection. "We're making magic coming together I'm telling you."

They both smile and lean closer while watching the sun set out over the ocean.

On their fifth hour, Garth and Jagger stroll home since both of their places are nearby and within walking distance.

They turn the corner onto Jagger's street both quiet and telepathically picking up on what the other is thinking and feeling.

"Should I walk you home now?" Jagger jokes and then gets serious, "It was so great to finally get to hang out with you and talk and get to know you."

"Same here." Garth smiles, "Can I see you again? I'm sure I'll run into you, but I mean, you know I very much

178

want to see you. Go out on another date and another and another." Garth laughs. "And do what we did today."

Jagger nods trying not to show too much excitement or be too carried away. He had been hurt enough over guys that suddenly disappear and drop off the radar. They felt it was he who wasn't interested in them. He never showed or had complete interest, and this was visibly obvious to them. This was different. Garth is different. "Yeah, I want to see you too, definitely."

Garth says, "Hope this isn't too sudden, but maybe I'll stop by tomorrow?"

"I'd love that." Jagger's body fills with excitement, "Maybe we can start the day with some surfing."

Garth laughs, "I'm game man."

CHAPTER 18

Jagger and Garth: Growing Closer

The next day Garth shows up at Jagger's door with his surfboard. Jagger has his surfboard and they head down to the shore together.

On another day they jog and stop to hang out on the beach on the jungle gym. Garth works on his pull-ups. Jagger shakes his head urging him to come down so he can show him how it's done. Jagger jumps up and begins to do pull ups, but Garth jumps up fast and pulls him down playfully tackling him.

They spend the next couple of weeks hanging out and going out and having a beautiful time. On one of the dates, Jagger shows up at the lifeguard tower Garth works at. Garth races out smiling and jumping off of it landing in front of him to steal a kiss.

One candlelit date night they dine together at a restaurant on the beach. Garth draws a heart on his napkin and slides it towards Jagger. Afterwards they both walk home together telepathically picking up on what the other is thinking and feeling. They arrive in front of Jagger's place.

Garth says, "Mate these last couple of weeks have been the time of my life and I love where this is going."

Jagger deliberates looking away. He doesn't want to get hurt anymore, but is slowly letting his guard down, "Yeah me too."

Garth gets him and leans into his ear. "I am not like those other guys Jagger. I'm not going anywhere." He runs his hand behind Jagger's neck giving it a tender squeeze followed by a luscious passionate kiss. He rests his forehead on Jagger's forehead comfortably.

Jagger smiles, "I know."

"Good. Do you want to come over to my place tomorrow night and hang out? Have a go at a quiet evening?"

"Fuck yeah," Jagger pulls back, "How about coming over to my place first?" It had been one of his rules to never let a guy come to his place. It would imply that things would get too serious. It had brought on more problems than he was inclined to want to deal with. Garth knew where he lived anyway. This was an exception to break one of his rules.

They smile at each other like silly in love teens. "I'll be coming over tomorrow then."

They back away from each other slowly not breaking eye contact. Garth slips his hands into his pockets as he makes the trek up the sidewalk out of view back home. Jagger watches him walk away wanting to check him out when he's not looking. Garth suddenly turns around with a huge smile to look at Jagger, "I'll see you later."

Jagger smiles, "Bye, Garth."

Jagger walks inside his place in a daze of euphoria. He throws his keys down and plops down on the couch. "Yes! Fuck yes!" He sits back thinking about Garth, the traces of his face and his body, the twitches and every little amazing thing about him. He's so in love with his personality and his soul. He imagines him naked, but loving that they have not had sex yet. The wait is silently killing the both of them, but they don't mind. They're too into one another to want to do it just yet. They've been purposely withholding as so many have sex right away and then the connection ends not long afterwards. This duo has too much love and respect for the other. And they know the sex will that much hotter when they do move into physical affection.

CHAPTER 19

Jagger and Garth: Twin Flame Love.

Music plays throughout Jagger's pad an hour or so after the date ended. He loves constant music, whether its low or loud is all good. He's barefoot and his jeans hang over his ass. There is a knock on his door. Wondering who that could be he answers it. His face lights up at who is on his doorstep.

Garth stands smiling and his dimples form at the tips of the sides of his lips. His eyes are bright and dilated with love. He hands over a flower. "Is it tomorrow?" Garth has on khaki beige pants and a black tank top that accentuate his muscles and body. The dude had gone home to shower and change.

Jagger takes the flower. "Holy shit no way. Thank you." He reaches over and grabs Garth by the front of his shirt. Garth's flirtatious and naughty smirk is in place. Jagger pulls him inside. "Get in here."

Garth towers over him like a bully and a crafty dog with good intentions. He leans in and kisses Jagger's lips gentle and long.

Jagger puts his hand up and backs away. "Make yourself at home and kick off your shoes. My place is your place now."

"Awesome." Garth looks around with a smile kicking off his flip-flops.

"Feel free to change the music if you want." Jagger heads into the kitchen.

Garth makes his way over to the stereo looking over the music selections.

Jagger brings a tribal vase into the room.

Garth pops in some smooth grooves music. He continues to steal eye contact from Jagger with a smile as if he were reading from a hot, sexy book and catching his stare whenever he would hit a naughty word. Jagger can't keep his eyes off him unable to believe the guy is in his living room. He is in complete and sheer amazement.

"Do you know that I can't remember anyone giving me a flower before?" Jagger says.

"You? You're joking. I don't believe that." Garth smiles wide.

Jagger shoots a look at him. "Seriously, no one here is as romantic and gesture giving as you might think. At least no one I've met. Something this world needs some definite help with."

"Nah-I can believe that man. The romance is dead here no?"

"It certainly seems to be that way wherever I look." Jagger sets the vase down and studies the flower. "This is much appreciative. You've floored me again."

Garth roams around the living room scoping out the place. He spots the Maori figure, "Whoa!"

"Yeah, it's my form of a stick God I guess."

"This is awesome!" Garth feels even more connected to him than before. He's falling in love over their similarities.

Jagger's finger traces lightly over Garth's tattoo. "I see you're protected by the Gods as well."

Garth's eyes pierce into him. "Ace mate. We're both watched over."

"Did you and I fight in another lifetime?" Jagger asks.

"Probably, but neither of us won. Garth grabs Jagger again giving him a loving squeeze, "We had to surrender to each other."

"That we have done." Jagger backs away a significant distance nervous being completely alone with him in close quarters. He starts to adjust the flower in the vase with the other flowers in it. He wants to do anything to keep his mind off the uneasiness.

The living room has low lighting and is rugged at night like in a mountain cabin. There are a few candles lit around the place. The sliding door to the balcony is open to a degree. The warm night breeze blows in enveloping the love intensity that is building at an expedited rate. There is an illumination from the moonlight outside which oddly makes a near cross on the wall.

The music starts up and Garth heads towards Jagger barefoot quickly with complete and devouring intention. Jagger jolts surprised and afraid to move drunk with love. Garth slows down in front of him and they sway without touching. They face each other alone and checking each other out. Garth discovers the tremble in Jagger's hand. Jagger takes in the shape of Garth's muscles, particularly the two monstrous ones that peer out like massive passion fruit.

Garth moves towards him deliberately with each centimeter feeling as if he's travelling a mile. Jagger is in a drunken love stupor. He observes Garth's full lips, his face, his body and his hands as well as the quiet traces of hair on his arm. His eyes fill with sensation and he falls over in a daze. He cuts abruptly back to reality only when Garth's lips nearly hit his. They don't make it to them before Jagger pulls away shaking his head with a strange ability to not accept anything. "Fuck! Sorry, I...Fuck." He lets out a nervous laugh and backs away another step and his back hits the wall behind him.

Garth isn't afraid of him and the edges of his smile pierce the sides of his lips. He moves towards him cautious as if to capture a wild animal. Jagger stands in slight fear and skittishness. He looks at him and feels his worthy intentions and is suddenly empowered. Garth eases into Jagger's personal space with his eyes never leaving his. With all the fire intensity burning off their bodies they both take one quick step towards each other. They lean in fast forming the position to kiss, stopping in mid air with anticipation for a second or two. The room feels as if its spinning around them at great speed when their lips energetically merge with one another.

Their mouths open for their tongues to meet and explore and discover treasure. Garth's arms skillfully find its way around Jagger tight pulling him against him.

Jagger's hands run up the side of Garth, bringing all the blood to the surface of his skin heating the guy up. He glides his hands onto Garth's forearms. Garth presses his body up against Jagger's hard.

Jagger leans forward into Garth's ear. "I want you." His breath on Garth's ear drives him nuts.

Garth's hands make its way down to the bulging part between Jagger's legs. *Hello.* He tugs on his earlobe a bit with his teeth at the same time. *Oh Mama Mia.*

Jagger's lips move towards Garth's ear. He sucks on his lobe and down his neck. Garth's face buries into Jagger's shoulder feeling weak in the knees. Jagger sucks on his neck affectionately for several minutes. Garth moves his hands up and down over Jagger's back and down over his ass. He hangs out there for a while to grab hold of what he claims as now his.

Garth presses his mouth against Jagger's slowly parting his lips by running his tongue along the edges hungry for him. His tongue pushes in and they make out for minutes delving into every part of their bodies. Garth's tongue reaches into Jagger's mouth feeling his soul.

They assertively kiss and make out in the corridor in the hall. They pull back for air staring into each other's eyes. Jagger's hand finds its way into Garth's hand leading him to the bedroom entry where he stops. They stay there making out for another few more minutes. Someone is going to have to pry them apart. Garth pulls Jagger into a hug and then another kiss. Jagger's deep big eyes shoot through every cell in Garth's body reading him.

Garth pulls Jagger into the bedroom and jumps on the bed like a child. Jagger crawls on over to him. Garth puts his hands onto Jagger's face whole and kisses him.

Garth's shirt rises up a little and Jagger teases his cut lines, the vertical creases on his mid body. Garth goes out of his mind when Jagger's hands dip down to his inner thighs.

Garth electrifies Jagger when he lifts up his shirt and climbs under it. He plants light kisses all up and down his body. He buries his head underneath his shirt, pinning him down on his back for a couple of minutes loving him.

Jagger locks his body around Garth's taller bigger body holding the sides of it with his hands. Garth leans over and gently rubs the small of Jagger's back feeling him up like a teenager. He plants wet delicious kisses on his chest erotically. Jagger gives attention to every part of his body tingling Garth's whole being.

Garth works Jagger's stomach and then chest before he tears Jagger's shirt off. Jagger follows and pulls Garth's off placing his hands up his body soaking it up. Garth reaches over and gives Jagger naughty bites on his inner thighs and the sides of his abs and then around on his back.

They give each other long burning kisses while rolling around on the bed misbehaving. Jagger pushes Garth on his back. Garth's hand and arm don't let go of him while Jagger leans down and plants butterfly kisses down the hairline between Garth's belly button and lower abs. Garth groans, "Oh man you're fucking torture. Don't stop!" Jagger chuckles nervously and reaches his hand over Garth's bicep and holding it while he kisses his body.

They roll around on the bed intertwined with each other. Jagger can feel Garth's massive hard on pressing against him from underneath his pants. Jagger unbuttons Garth's pants a little. Garth jumps up and yanks his pants off leaving only his boxers on. Jagger's heart beat accelerates as he's seeing much more of Garth's naked body up close. Garth strips Jagger down to his boxers and kisses down his chest and stomach and then back up to his lips. He nips at Jagger's bottom lip, mixing a little roughness into their sweltering make-out love. They roll around on top of each other as the foreplay grows hotter and more intense. Jagger soaks in Garth's entire sexual raving body and cops a feel under his boxers, "Fuck yeah." He pulls Garth's boxers slowly down revealing his cock that is thick and huge with low hangars. His tan line is similar to his, which is what happens with most beach men and women.

Garth yanks and tears Jagger's boxers off abruptly watching his cock pop out. Garth grabs hold of Jagger's body with his strong hands. He leans over him and kisses his lips and his neck. He sows more kisses down all over his chest simultaneously pulling on his nipples, releasing every sensory titillation possible and driving Jagger mad. Jagger closes his eyes, then opens them to the wetness of his cock experiencing Garth's tongue being run down the side of it. Garth slides the cock into his mouth, pulling it out and sliding his tongue down the side of it again, then sliding Jagger's cock back into his mouth while he massages his balls with his hand.

Jagger puts his hands on Garth's torso prompting him to move up to where he wants him to go. Garth's cock slides into Jagger's mouth. He tastes sweetly amazing and the thickness grows in his mouth even more. Garth watches Jagger do this and grows excited to see his love give him affection in a sexual way. Jagger flicks his tongue against the tip of Garth's cock and then takes him in his mouth. The feeling is as intense for Garth as he cries out nearly falling over.

They move back to kiss passionately as if they have found their long lost love. Their uncontrolled naked bodies press up against each other with their legs interlinked in the process. Garth tells Jagger that he wants it with him.

Jagger pulls away with a smirk reaching over to the drawer by the bed. He pulls out a condom packet and cups it. He runs it along the trail between Garth's stomach and pubic region.

Garth's face lights up cheery and high in love. "Come here."

Jagger gently pushes his cock in slow and occasional. He checks on Garth to make sure that he is okay and holds him close kissing him at the same time. Garth is stunned as it is the first time and he likes it. Jagger does it so that it feels good. Garth can't believe it and knows he can get used to this. Jagger makes love to him with affection as he penetrates him with his cock.

Their bodies mesh together perfect experimenting like virgins. Garth holds onto Jagger prompting him to fuck rapid like an animal. He thrusts in and out of him hard.

Garth's hands move down over Jagger's back and over the bottom of his ass holding his hands there. This makes Jagger fuck him faster. Garth is set up in flames and forcefully pushes his tongue into Jagger's mouth at the same time. Garth massages Jagger's chest, his hands moving up and down it to the horny beat of the humping.

Hours of hot fucking, scorching foreplay and endless lovemaking go by. Jagger cries out, "Fuck!" He pulls out and ejaculates. Garth holds the back of his neck with his strong hand. Almost simultaneously, Garth climaxes shooting his cum out which hits Jagger's body. Garth leans up and kisses Jagger hard both creating unbelievable sensory overload that neither have experienced.

They both don't stop at the after play. They kiss sweetly running their hands very lightly over each other's body.

"Wow!" Garth shouts. "You are fucking incredible. Oh my." He smiles and falls on Jagger curling up with him for a few minutes.

The jets shoot out water in Jagger's little spa tub in the bathroom. Jagger finishes lighting the candles placed around it. They climb in and Garth leans back onto Jagger who envelops him with his legs. Jagger massages the back of Garth's neck, shoulders and arms.

Garth moans low, "My muscles are so sore. I need your help."

Jagger smiles and digs his hands into Garth's muscles and chuckles. "I bet." He lets his fingers trickle along

Garth's back. He leans down and kisses the area under the back of his neck.

Garth smiles wide and speaks low. "Come here you." Jagger leans his head around and Garth's head propels forward nabbing onto Jagger's lips kissing him. "Mmm. Nice."

Jagger wraps a towel around Garth holding it around him. Garth leans in and plants a kiss.

"You can put on one of my boxers if you want to stay here tonight." Jagger says.

"Or we can sleep naked together." Garth smiles.

"I love the way you think!" Jagger pulls a pair of boxers out of the closet and hands them to him. They are a little tight on Garth, but look incredibly hot on him. They both fix up the bed they messed up together propping up the pillows smiling while stealing teenage lust-filled glances. Both finish standing on opposite sides of the bed with hotter enticing looks than they had ever given. They've reached a more settling comfort level between one another.

They jump sudden with Jagger's knee gently landing on one side of the bed and Garth's on the other side facing each other. They both crawl on the bed towards each other. Their lips land where they are born to be. They kneel on the bed exploring each other's soft bodies up against each other. They laugh at how surreal their coming together is. They dreamt it, wished it, manifested it and now it's become a reality. They grab the blanket together and pull it down climbing underneath the covers.

"This is so fucking trippy as shit." Jagger says.

"I love your voice." Garth says too happy knowing Jagger is playing like he didn't hear him. "Did you hear what I said?"

"Yeah," Jagger says, "You like my voice."

"It's rough right now and you sound even sexier." A grin from ear to ear plasters on Garth's face.

"I'm tired. It's that late night voice."

"Mmm, well it's sexy, get over here and sleep on me." Garth urges on.

"Fuck, don't tempt me."

They both instantaneously move in super close. Their hands reach to grab hold of what belongs to them now. They've marked their territories.

Garth wraps his strong, loving arms tightly around Jagger. "Being in each other's arms is fulfilling. I knew you would be a great lover. Me? I knew I would be staring in your eyes 24/7. They tell me so much about you." He leans in kissing Jagger's forehead. "Honey, when I'm not here, never a night will go by that I won't have your picture on the pillow beside me. It's the next best thing to have us filling our arms locked together. Feeling your body pressing against me and our lips falling in everlasting kisses." He leans in to kiss Jagger again.

"Getting to see what's inside your inner thoughts makes me smile." Jagger says, "You can tell me anything. I am wide open for you."

They lie in each other's arms staring at each other and at the ceiling with happy smirks.

"Perhaps one day you can write me a love story on how the greatest man in the U.S. fell in love with a simple Aussie guy. We could have quite a torrid affair, very tempting too. Man, I'm like jello in your arms and I love feeling you." Garth's hands wander over Jagger's body. "Hell I'm going to tear those clothes off every chance I get!"

"Well, you can and you better!"

"Picture it: We would make headlines. Hey, U.S. columnist and Aussie guy caught naked in beach lounge."

Jagger laughs. "Damn, I love your fantasy. I love feeling you. Feeling what it's like to lay next to you. Finally getting to look into your eyes and talk to you. I'm enamored by you, curious about you and drawn to you in many ways."

Garth kisses him over and over down onto his chest and his body. "Mmm, babe, let me kiss you from head to toe, but will probably never get past your cock." He quickly pulls Jagger's boxers slightly down a bit slamming a kiss below his navel.

"Come on man." Jagger says getting playful.

"I want it deep in my throat. I want to taste the essence of your love." Garth gazes back up at Jagger in heavy flirtation. "I can think of no great act, but us 69-ing together, totally pleasuring each other until we can't hold out any longer, then flooding each other with our cum."

"Oooo baby. Ssssss. Now you're acting like me."

Garth laughs, "Nah you don't know, man. I want you, always have. I want to belong to you totally. I want us to be one person and proud of the fact that we're together. You're going to be my main bloke."

Jagger confesses. "I've experienced things in my life that now that I look back never seemed possible to ever have happened. I want to show you my love too. I want to brag about it. I want you to experience it. When you talk to me and I hear what's pouring out of your heart, it's as if you're slowly fucking me. It's the best."

"Damn!" Garth rolls his body on top of Jagger and kisses him all over, "Man. You make me feel like the most important guy in the world. I'm glad we have connected physically. I feel that much closer to you. I like that I'm going to be waking up to you tomorrow morning. We will never get any sleep."

"I'm comfortable with you I will sleep." Jagger confesses.

"I've moved your soul." Garth says.

"And with me it's like moving a mountain."

They fall into another long kiss.

The planted kisses are fewer and fewer as they both travel off to sleep in each other's arms, drifting and into the best slumber either have had.

In the middle of the night, Garth wakes up and notices they are both cuddling. While both half asleep, Garth disappears under the covers and softly kisses Jagger's body all over his chest and down his stomach.

Sometimes when you begin to see a new person, all those past bad experiences have an opportunity to be banished. You get to start fresh and create something better with this new person. You have a clean slate. You're more experienced than before and you get better at it each time. Letting other people lead the way is not such a bad thing.

Feeling restless in the middle of the night, Garth gets up and paces a bit. He looks around for a sheet of paper and a pen in the room. He sits down to write his thoughts down in a letter. Letter writing is the best way to grab someone you truly like. Garth naturally knows what Jagger would like. He lights the candle that is on the desk and sits by the soft light that accentuates his beautiful, strong body. He occasionally looks over at Jagger who is asleep, then back to the paper and up ahead as he thinks and writes.

The next morning Garth's eyes open. He's lying on his back and looks down. A smile creeps over his face. His cock is thick and growing erect. Jagger is dead asleep with half his body on Garth's. Garth moves in and wraps his arms and legs around Jagger getting a feel of his hot dude's ass. Jagger's eyes start to open forgetting for a second that Garth is there. He comes to and then grows his cocky, hot smirk. A guy had spent the night.

Garth looks over and then rocks Jagger in his arms and in his morning gravelly voice, "G'morning me love."

"Hey." Jagger utters unable to say more. He's too tired, but not tired enough to show it through physical love. His arm and body reach around Garth tight in a love embrace.

"Mmm, I love being enveloped by you." Garth says. "Get over here!" He pulls him in tighter.

Garth's erection grows more. Jagger grabs Garth's hand gently darting his tongue against his palm in an erotic way. He knows it's working because Garth's cock is solid wood and jabs the side of him. Jagger's cock grows in succession and pokes out of his boxers a little. Garth uses one of his hands to stick it down Jagger's boxers and caress his cock.

Jagger plants kisses over Garth's chest. Garth wraps around him even tighter. He sucks on Jagger's ear lobe a little, then down to his lips taking in slow kissing suctions. They move in at the same time with hot morning foreplay, making out and then pulling the other's boxers off for more scorching lovemaking. They kiss naked while stopping to connect with each other's eyes.

Jagger looks at him and rubs Garth's arm. "Last night was the bomb. You were fucking awesome and you tasted good."

Garth is gleeful loving it, "Bomb. Awesome. Good. Yeah. That would be you. Sexy eyes. Great smile. Incredible personality. So don't know what to do with it!"

Hours later they put their clothes on to head to the "Beached Hut." They want to show each other off.

Garth walks around in his pants, barefoot like his counterpart. Jagger pulls a shirt out of his closet for Garth and walks over to him from behind resting his hand on Garth's back. "You didn't bring a change of clothes, try this one maybe."

Garth smiles and lets Jagger slip the shirt on him, one arm after the other. Jagger reaches his arms around him pressing his body against Garth's from behind, "Fuck, you feel good." Garth smiles excited with his hand clasped into Jagger's.

Jagger continues to button up the shirt from the front while he holds him.

Garth shakes his head going out of his mind. He had never met anyone or been with anyone who was loving, seductive and strong at the same time. "Man, you dressing me makes me want to strip my clothes off!"

Jagger smiles, "Taking your clothes off is hot, but putting them on you is even hotter. I get it. We'll have plenty of opportunities for that I'm sure."

Garth turns around with a smile to face him. "We most definitely will."

Jagger half smiles smoothing out the creases on the front of Garth's shirt focusing on the detail like an attentive spouse. He looks up to lock eyes with the intense in love stare he is receiving from Garth. "There you are my love. Perfect. You're ready for your close up."

Garth leans his head down slightly to lock into a sensual kiss with Jagger and then grabs him to hold for a beat. Garth lifts Jagger's shirt up and kisses his chest. Jagger's hands rest on his shoulders. Garth leans back up to kiss him on the lips. They pull away and leave the house. Garth quickly turns around, "Oh wait!" He yanks something out of his pocket. Turning around with his eyes lowered and his fingers a poem, he hands Jagger his folded note.

Jagger shakes a little trembled by the gift. "Breaking up with me already, are ya?" He jokes.

"Never. Put this in your pocket though. Don't read it now. Read it later when we're out and you're not around me, otherwise I'll get embarrassed."

True love doesn't go away. You can't put it under a rock or any other place. It can't be denied or hidden away. You can't find a way to understand it especially if you've never experienced it yourself.

Rays of stars shine out in plain view during the day, which is impossible in a city like L.A. Garth grabs Jagger's hand and clasps it tight leaning his body towards him. "You are a beauty." He squeezes it tightly. "Oh and babe, not just on the outside, but especially on the inside too."

The right person for you will recognize your greatest qualities. It's nothing that can be forced. When someone amazing moves your soul, then they are rewarded with the best you both have to offer. They see the flaws as attractive and that's when you've hit a gold mine.

The love duo arrive at the place where they had their first date.

Garth jumps ahead when they walk in. He announces that he's going to get them a table with a view and will bring back some non-alcoholic drinks.

The music blares up loud and Jagger pulls out the letter from Garth dying of curiosity to read what it says. His eyes move over it with hot sentiment. He smiles then moves into a serious deadpan.

Dear Jagger,

Woke in the middle of the night in a dream about you and had this one massive hard on. I'm in your room with you and you are fast asleep and looking like a stud. We spent last night fucking and making love for hours. Every time I look at you I see love in those eyes. Love for whom, I don't know, but sure is great thinking it might be for me. I want to see right down into your soul, to see your inner most thoughts, and see if they are about me.

I want to kiss you from head to toe, but would probably never get past your cock. I want it deep in my throat. I want to taste the essence of your love.

I want to write a story about you babe, but it would never be allowed to print. I wouldn't be able to keep it clean. Damn you make my thoughts turn to pure lust. Before this, it was sure hell loving a man I thought I couldn't get, but look, I'm in his bedroom. I can't even believe it.

I want to make love to that body of yours and connect to your soul. I lust for you man, your lips, your chest, your cock, your balls and your ass. I hate the idea of some other guy taking what is mine!

I've seen you for a long time and watched you and I'm not afraid to say any of this. You are the last thing I want to see at night and the first in the morning. I want you with me. I want to make you fall in love with me, make you want me for your own, live our lives together, maybe have kids. I know you might think this is misplaced puppy dog love or maybe that I just fancy your look and your body. This isn't true. Yes, I love those things, but what I love about you is deeper than that. I love who you are, your personality and everything about you. I'll stand by your side man. I feel it and I know it's always been you.

Honey, wish you would write a story about me, about some stupid Aussie who loves this American stud columnist who would do anything to have him on his terms. Can you imagine how much I love you? Yet you probably think me some dumb Aussie guy.

You are the other half of me, without you, I am not complete. Man, I sit here in your room writing this looking over at you fast asleep, so cute! I wonder how I am fortunate to meet a guy like you. Believe me I do see inside your mind. I see a man that anybody would desire and want for his own without any hesitation.

You bring out the best in me. I want to be perfect for you and at the same time I want to strip your clothes off and possess you in every possible way. I want to be inside you, to make love to you, to kiss your body and hold you close. I want you to be the man in my life, to make me whole.

I dream about you writing about our love and yet can't see the finale. Can't see what the future holds. Maybe I should concentrate on getting past the sexual adventures. Maybe you can help with the ending and make it real.

I can't believe that you have not a mile of potential lovers all lined up waiting for the chance to be yours. You seduce me with the glance of your eyes and yet you're passionate and gentle.

I had looked for you on the beach often, but you were never there. My heart always jumped at the thought of talking to you, but whenever I saw you I'd suddenly get shy. I thought this guy will shoot me down. I want to read your words Jagger to know how you feel, to *know your thoughts, to know your body as well as your mind. I will always be yours, even if not as a lover, husband, partner, but as a friend, whatever you choose. You have my whole being and I want you to be my main bloke.*

Yours,

Garth.

Jagger pulls the note away taking a deep breath. "Jesus." He shakes his head exhaling. He is shaky and dizzy, feeling like he might fall over. His head is light and his eyes flood a little with rare mist. Garth's words are exceptionally intense. The hot-blooded implication to his note is ardent. It is poured right out of his heart like a geyser. Jagger soars into an ecstatic awakening. He wants to surrender to a new beginning that is proposed to him. Every part of his body shines at Garth's suggestions. They are both equally on the same footing when it comes to the deep meaning of love and sex.

It isn't that either don't have potential lovers in Los Angeles, but L.A. is a different place. The guys and girls tend to be less relationship driven than them. Relationships in L.A. end as quickly as they begin. Attention spans are brief and fleeting. Jagger's not good at giving his love to anybody. When he gives his love it's strong and lasting. He's in it for the long haul. Love is in front of him. He has an opportunity to jump on a real train and for once he knows this is right. It isn't shallow or irrelevant. There is no bullshit air about it. He doesn't put his armor up. He can let his guard down and let someone real in. This is someone who displays genuine and bold intentions. If Garth had been hurt before, he didn't allow it to stop him from going after Jagger. Jagger is someone that Garth wants. It will not stop Jagger from meeting him half way.

Garth approaches Jagger from behind. He is lit up and moves his hand up the side of Jagger's body. He wraps it around the front of him. Jagger can feel his breath on his neck.

The music moves into a chorus and Jagger abruptly turns around. His face and his eyes fill with mystery. Garth shakes a little when he sees the letter opened in Jagger's hand. He pauses unsure if Jagger is put off by it.

The butterflies swim in Jagger's stomach as well as Garth's. They are in deep love. Jagger feels as if he had spent his whole life to get to him. Garth watches him worried and puzzled.

"You wrote this for me?" Jagger holds the letter up.

"Yeah, was that okay? I had to tell you mate. I know it might've been too soon, but I meant every word love and I wanted you to know. I've pulled every piece of linen off the table. I don't keep things like that hidden when I know there's something there." Garth looks deep into Jagger, "I hope it was okay."

"Baby, you better fucking believe it's okay." Jagger's smile grows wider than it ever has. "Come here."

Garth's eyes fall into a spell with his. Jagger slides his hand strong up Garth's arm and around his back. Garth grabs him intensely and wraps his whole self around him. Their lips lock and the music flares up to a boom. The whole place rocks and spins around them while other's glance at them envious and joyful with what the two have officially initiated.

~~The End~~
THE BEGINNING

Jagger & Garth

SCENES FROM A
REVOLUTIONARY ROMANCE

The following pages contain assorted sample scenes involving Jagger and Garth. Where are they now? They are in the beginning stages of a relationship that is bathed in love, companionship and mutual respect. This is for those craving a little extra on this hot couple. Random glimpses into how the honeymoon stage is going for them in this bonus chapter section.

SCENES FROM A
REVOLUTIONARY ROMANCE

Jagger's Journal Entry:

My husband recently came into my life this past year. His name is Garth, the one that was in my prophetic dream. He is an Australian and lives around the corner from me. I've had a crush on him since I first saw him walk past my house to head down to the beach a couple of years ago. When I first saw him I thought, "This is the guy." It wasn't the kind of this is him I've ever said before.

Garth is a giving person with a great sense of humor. He is easy to talk to, open-minded, and does not judge others, even when he feels completely the opposite of what they believe. He is in great shape and takes good care of himself. He watches his health and gets a good deal of exercise. He's a music and movie lover, and appreciates documentaries. He is a great listener and can talk for hours if he connects well with someone. I went through a lot of bad Knights before I graduated to something out of this world. This was before I knew that I was ready. My whole body trembles with butterflies in every cell when it comes to Garth. Never mind that he's a babe, but a direct descendant of a King. Leave it to me to attract in royalty. I have a pretty good Prince Charming I have to say, but this ain't fucking disney and nor is it a fairy tale. Still – it's closer to anything I've ever had before.

As I got to know him, I knew I could give him something too. I'm not going to sit back and relax and let a dude pamper me while I suck it up. I'm practical and love goes both ways.

I was recently watching a romantic movie clip I needed to inspire me to write a column, but five minutes in I got irritated and shut it off. I thought, "I don't need to see this. I have that romance in my life now." Man someone should put that on a tea bag. That's some wise shit. It's always been inside you.

JAGGER AND GARTH SCENES:

Garth dances around his place to his blasting music. He laughs having a great time alone. He pulls his cell phone out grinding his hip. He scrolls down to Jagger's name and types him a text: "I miss you, love you and want you."

Jagger sees it, picks it up and smiles. He texts him back: "I miss you too love. =)"

Garth lights up when he reads it. He clenches his fist and can't contain himself wanting to text him some more. "I want you now. When can I see you please? Hurry I'm dying over here. ☺ ☺ ☺"

Jagger smirks exhaling afraid to give in, but smiling at the same time. He likes it, but doesn't want to get hurt. He knows this is the guy. Garth loves that he could be that guy. It's what he's wanted too. They have date night at least once a week no matter what. It might be dinner and/or a movie.

Jagger types him back, "Come on over.   I'm

waiting."

Garth shows up at Jagger's door wearing his beach khaki's. His golden dirty blonde hair glistens, "Hey babe, I got us some...." His eyes light up and he salivates, then licks his lips, "...got us some treats."

Garth kicks the door closed. Jagger walks over barefoot messes up Garth's hair a little reaching over for the bag, but not before Garth yanks the bag away and lowers to steal a kiss from him first.

Garth drops the DVD's on the coffee table and says: "Some romance flicks. I know how much you're a sucker for that shit." He adds. "It's background baby while we lay on the couch necking each other all night. We're going to watch them and feel them together."

Jagger and Garth give each other a quick kiss on the lips.

"Don't worry, I also have a scary one so you can latch onto me and I can feel your heart beating like a little rabbit." He grabs Jagger's waist playfully.

Garth has his bow and arrow aiming it at the sun manifesting his mate. What more could you expect from a Sagittarius. He has to aim for the hottest burning intensity. Jagger is an Aries with a lot of grounding Earth signs in the mix, which explains why he's ferociously defending his turf.

They are the quintessential fire couple, darting from place to place conquering the world. At the end of the day of battling the jungle, they retreat to each other with some real hot erotic lovemaking. Kissing in the morning as their love prompts them to go after the world even harder. Sexually they're over the top, full of fun with a similar sense of humor.

Garth was the High School football quarterback while growing up in Australia. He then made a move to playing rugby when he got into a couple years of College. Afterwards he moved to L.A. and became a lifeguard. He's begun training to eventually become a Fireman. He loves to 'rescue' and help. His football days taught him the value and importance of teamwork, which would later be vital in him being able to contribute positively to the endurance of a REAL relationship.

Jagger and Garth lay down on the floor in front of a big screen TV in the entertainment room. The floor is immaculate and comfortable. They are on sleeping bags like they're on a camping trip. They are wrapped around one another like snakes to a vine. Jagger doesn't even care about the movie. He likes feeling Garth's lips occasionally pressing against his throughout the film.

Sometimes Garth likes to walk around in his lifeguard shorts with no shirt. He's got his hands in his pockets while he strolls through Jagger's little backyard alone reflecting.

Jagger is inside throwing food in the oven. He reaches for his ringing phone. He can't believe he's doing this shit. But he knows he found his soul mate and doesn't want to blow it.

Later that night, Jagger sits up in bed typing his next column on his laptop. Garth is spread out over the bed working on his web fighter project in his notebook. Jagger looks on perplexed and Garth notices.

Garth smiles, "What babe?"

"Can't believe you're here. I mean you're fucking here."

Garth rises up a little, "Believe it." He leans in to kiss Jagger taking all of his lips in, sweetly pushing his tongue into his mouth. "Come here." He reaches over taking the laptop from Jagger and putting it aside. He grabs him and pulls Jagger up on top of him.

Two people sleeping together in a bed is the most intimate time of the day for them, because no one else is around. It's their one moment where they can truly and honestly be personal. Everyone wants a love partner, but once you have them, then the real challenge begins. Now there is another element in your life, a new and important one. They want to be a part of you and know what you're thinking, what you're doing, and how you're doing. You were used to being untouched, alone, and holding your pillow at night. Now there is a handsome prince next to you and he wants your soul. It's work to release yourself to someone else, but how much of it do you release?

Garth likes to channel surf and Jagger is anti-television, but who should give up what they love doing? This is who Garth is and this is who Jagger is and they both should hold dear to what they separately love. Compromise is a key factor in a relationship. There are certain things you're going to give up, because you will never meet anyone who is exactly like you. If you believe you've met someone who is, then you better look closer, because that person doesn't exist. It's impossible for him to be a carbon copy of yourself.

People have their idiosyncrasies and the pet peeves. If the thought of that makes you cringe, then a relationship is not for you. You would do best to not pursue a dude in the hopes of a relationship with them when you already know you would never be willing to allow someone else's quirks into your life. It's being aware that one of you could be in a mood that you don't understand and it has nothing to do with you. It's being able to tell when to give them their space.

Jagger doesn't talk in the morning. Garth likes to talk. If there is anything they both love, it's to snuggle with each other in the middle of the night. They enjoy feeling close to each other and to be able to talk to each other about their darkest secrets no matter how twisted or perverted it might be. They have each other's open mind to what comes out.

Jagger wears boxers and combat boots. The muscles in his legs pulsate out as he jogs up the stairs to Garth's abode. He races through the place that has music pounding the walls. He walks into Garth's bathroom and grabs his mouthwash.

Garth finds Jagger in there rinsing with mouthwash. He comes up behind him and smacks him on the ass, "You are going to stay here tonight. You're going to get in my bed out there and you're going to like it."

Jagger sneers, partially turned on by it, but also not feeling comfortable with someone trying to dominate him. Yet - he rather enjoys it too, "Since you put it that way." Jagger's voice cracks with rough edges and he goes back to rinsing and brushes past him.

Garth grabs him with force and pins him up against the doorframe and licks and kisses the side of his neck.

Jagger is unable to move, but excited.

Garth sucks on Jagger's ear lobe pulling away slowly, "Mmmm." He smacks and grabs his ass again, "Get in my bed. I own you dammit."

Garth disappears down the hall and Jagger suddenly

likes the feeling of someone else trying to take control for a change. He wrestles with getting too soft or passive because he's always been a tough ass. Love softens you.

Jagger walks into the room seeing Garth lounging across the bed reading the "Wall Street Journal". Garth is now wearing glasses that make him appear sexier than he's ever been, and that's already hard to do. Garth looks up with a smirk," What's up babe?"

Jagger shrugs it off confused, "Nothing." He puckers his lips in angst.

Garth is reading intently. Now they're a married couple. Jagger thinks, "I could get into this". He slowly lifts up the blankets edging in trying to make himself less nervous that he's not in his own surroundings. He had wanted someone to go the distance with, but now that he has it he doesn't know how to handle it.

Garth picks up on this and throws the paper to the floor and proceeds to crawl over Jagger like an animal with a dangerous smile. He stares down at Jagger and they both get embarrassed and laugh looking the opposite ways.

"This is all new to me." Jagger says.

Garth shakes his head agreeing, "Oh boy do I know." Continuously smiling he pulls his glasses off and places them on the end table. He shakes his hair like a wet dog. Jagger reaches up grabbing a hold of him by it gently. Garth mimics the howl of a dog and moves his lips over Jagger's. He lightly brushes his lips over Jagger's, then starts kissing him. He pushes his tongue into Jagger's mouth and then his lips over Jagger's and over again. Garth stops and gets a little serious, "I saw the prints of that new ad they're putting you in." His dimples show through his smile. "Very sexy. Almost very naked."

Jagger scoffs at the external attention, "It's all marketing stuff for the columns and my first book that's coming out. You know that."

"You are a silly boy. Please keep your pants on. I will be so jealous if anybody were to see my baby's wee-wee hanging out the bottom of his shorts." Garth shakes off his jealousy for a minute, "It's so weird, but I find myself getting jealous. I can't explain. I feel a connection to you. I hope I don't turn you off spilling my heart out. When I have a boyfriend I get jealous, territorial, and feel the need to protect him. I'm getting those feelings toward you these days. I hope I don't scare you off with these words. I just need to get them out. I think you are the perfect man. Alright, alright I'll shut up."

Jagger laughs and grabs him, "I love being protected by you and you don't have anything to be jealous of. That's all work you know that, but I am all yours and belong to you only." Jagger kisses him affectionately and Garth falls into it, but then pulls away leaving Jagger concerned.

Garth gets up and strolls over to the bedroom window expressing uncomfortable feelings. "I have no control over who likes you. You are an amazing person and it's very easy to see why people gravitate toward you. I'd be lying if I didn't say I do get jealous feelings, but that is my problem. I know in reality fate has taken over and we've become a couple. I realize that I will spend most of my time fighting off the herds of men and I know some women who are wanting a piece of my baby. I am prepared for that."

Jagger forms half a smile, "Garth, I can assure you that they won't and can't hold a candle to you."

Garth looks out the bedroom window serious. "I am in a loving relationship with you and I give you all my love, all my soul, all my thoughts, and all my body. You have no reason to accept the advances of any other man. Okay, sorry if I'm rambling on or said too much, but I feel the need to say how I feel. I do turn some people off, hopefully not you."

Jagger walks up behind Garth and wraps his arms around him tightly. He kisses Garth's back lightly between his shoulder blades, "I understand you feeling concerned and I want you to feel comfortable enough to tell me when you do. This way I can reassure you that you have nothing to worry about." Garth smiles feeling comfortable again. Jagger rubs the sides of Garth's arms. "Damn your muscles are getting bigger these days and are intimidating me."

Garth lights up and turns around holding Jagger with them. "Why do they intimidate you babe? I have them so that each time I hug you, you will feel my arms and the emotion behind them." They kiss again.

On another day...

Jagger finds himself being hit with the jealousy bug or the curious bug anyway. He is investigating Garth's social networking page to see if he can find out any information. You know the kind you want to find out by someone you like. You hope you're only coming across good stuff that makes it look like he's only into you. At the very least, that he's not into anyone else.

Jagger powers up his laptop and types in the URL of Garth's page. He begins to quickly skim it for information, and is jolted when the music on the page blasts up super loud. He eyes the music player scrolling it to see if any of the songs are about him. The scrolling goes on for miles, before he's interrupted.

"Hello!" Garth's voice shouts coming down the hall.

It's Garth.

Fuck!

"Yes!" Jagger shouts nervously, "Hey! Be right out!"

Jagger tries to hit the pause button, slamming his mouse to hurry, but he realizes Garth is about to enter the bedroom. He impatiently clicks the mouse, but it freezes up. He slides his laptop with such force to the ground hoping it'll shut the music off so Garth doesn't find out.

"What's up here?" Garth eyes the laptop on the floor playing the song from his page. He runs down beating Jagger to it pulling it up. He sees it's his page. He looks up at Jagger who has his arms folded looking away like a scolded child.

Garth smiles with glee, loving that his man checks up on him. He finds it charming and tosses the laptop on the bed enveloping Jagger in his arms. He kisses him down his neck. "Come here cutie."

Jagger tries desperately to push him away embarrassed and then lets it happen. "Sorry I didn't know you were going to be here that soon. I'm…"

"What do you think you're gonna find huh? Huh baby? There's only you. You're gonna find nothin'." Garth continues to kiss him all over.

Kevin Hunter

Later that night…

Jagger holds Garth's hips with burning heat while he pounds his ass rock hard. His balls slap around hanging low while his cock penetrates him. Garth submissively uses his strong arms to pull Jagger towards him until they climax together. Instead of collapsing while they cum, Garth laughs and rolls Jagger onto his back and plants kisses on his neck which grow into smooth love bites. There's something about heated sex after discovering something that gets you hot and bothered about your lover.

Jagger writes in his journal:

I'm experiencing a heightened sense of confidence because that's what love does for you. I'm often hard on myself, analyzing my performance, my manner, and my achievements. Now I feel proud of all that I have accomplished. I'm on a track that will lead me to much greater success. I finally have the intuitive sense that all of the choices I have made have put me on the right path, one that includes love.

Love is when nothing is looked for in return. Love is when the tough gets tougher and the bond grows stronger. Love is treating your partner with constant respect even if you disrespect others. They are the one person that will value you and who you will hold with great esteem. Everything has changed quickly and you no longer need to rely on dozens to fill up your own unhappiness, now you have one.

I hope I don't blow it. It was a long, hard journey

215

to get to this place, to get the dude of my dreams. Fairy tale. Fiction. I know. Who gives a shit? I'm happy. He's here and he likes me. He likes me a lot. He's softened me. I was closed off and rigid before him. He teaches me things. Teaches me to have patience, to be less hard on others and myself, that's what a soul mate is. He is someone who makes you face the shit.

JAGGER AND GARTH SCENES:

Garth takes Jagger away for the weekend to a small cabin he's rented in the mountains. Jagger is outside and sees Garth coming back from his jog. The sweat races down Garth's chest, which holds his iPod wire like magnet to steel. His Maori tattoo clings to his bicep and glistens under the sunshine.

Jagger picks up Garth's football sitting on the lawn and tosses it to Garth.

Garth's clutches it and hurls it at Jagger, but misses hitting a couple of glass cups set out front.

"Oh shit mate." Garth exclaims.

Jagger laughs, "Don't worry about it. It's nothing."

"Fuck me dead." Garth smiles, "I don't know what I was thinking."

"That I could catch it." Jagger kids around nudging him lovingly.

Garth grabs Jagger's hand and pulls him towards him. They kiss and walk at the same time with their arm around each other like two pals crossing the line.

"It's my turn." Jagger explains, "I'm gonna head out

and get my own work out in for the day."

"Alright babe, I'll be here."

Garth goes inside and pulls long stem roses out of his bag and sticks them in all the furthest corners around the cabin. He places them in other areas outside like the hedges and mailbox and front door. He steps back away getting a good look and nods approvingly of himself.

Jagger arrives back at the cabin after his work out. He gleams noticing what Garth has been up to. He smiles pulling a rose out from the mailbox and moves through the cabin looking for him.

Garth is on the backyard patio deck lying down on a bench with his eyes closed. His body is muscular and tight. You can tell he works out more than regularly, but devotes his life to it. He still has is shorts made out of sweatpants on. You can see where he tore the bottoms off of it. His body is the product of hard work, eating right, and daily weight lifting.

Jagger is on the smaller scale. He's toned, but Garth looks like he could crush Jagger if he wanted to and sometimes he does!

Garth jolts awake as he feels Jagger gliding the rose across his chest. Garth grabs and tackles him playfully.

That night…

It's warm out enough that Garth has set up the TV onto the patio deck to watch: *"A Nightmare on Elm Street."* They share a rare tiny marijuana joint together.

The movie scares the shit out of Jagger because there is no one else around but them, the wild animals in the woods, and the Manson Family. The high exacerbates the scary feelings. Garth is roaming around on the deck staring out at the darkness enjoying the creepiness of the surrounding woods.

Jagger says to Garth, "How about you sit next to me please."

Garth laughs knowing Jagger is scared for a change. His plan worked. Garth heads over to sit next to him. He wraps his arm around Jagger pulling him against him.

Afterwards, they watch the animated movie, "*Finding Nemo*" to soften things. Jagger is not as tough as he normally is in the dark and wants something cute to play on the DVD player to wipe out the dark fear of the previous film. They don't watch Nemo anyway, but use that opportunity to make out and focus on each other while it plays in the background.

Jagger is vocal during sex at times. He is an enigma so it varies. He is not the same every time, but there's nothing like moaning and groaning with his guy.

Jagger majored in Communications with an emphasis in broadcast journalism. He was on his way to becoming a news anchor, but ended up being a sex columnist instead.

Garth is an only child, but is close to his parents. Unfortunately his mother passed away due to a long illness years before he moved to Southern California. She had a great life. Garth loves puppies, little kids laughter, the feeling after a great workout, or a great day of work makes him smile

Jagger doesn't drink coffee, never had a drop. It never appealed to him, but he drinks tea occasionally. He's more of a juice, water type of guy. No soda pop.

Garth is a huge fan of jazz, Chris Botti, Cassandra

Wilson, Praful, Ella Fitzgerald, Ramsey Lewis, Billie Holiday, some 70's soul music are some favorites. Jagger loves rock and roll like the Joan Jett song.

Garth knows his best features are his smile, chest and to be honest, he says his ass, which he states is a 'big ole muscle butt'. He wears boxer briefs because he likes the fit. Jagger is a boxer guy, but Garth sleeps nude and likes the way his pubes and cock feel against Jagger's bare skin.

Garth's close friends say that he is a great listener, non judgmental, and the 'most non-gay gay guy they know'. He would kiss a guy in the morning. He feels in a relationship that you see each other at your best and worst and a quick kiss in the morning wouldn't offend him. He is naturally smooth, not much body hair at all, except pubes, and he keeps them bushy because it's the only part of him that's hairy. He doesn't shave or trim. Garth's heroes are his dad, strongest and most giving person on earth. He also admires people who took a stand for their rights and others such as Rosa Parks.

Jagger & Garth's Video Diary

Jagger looks into the web camera set up and presses record:

"When I saw Garth I knew right away, this was it. I oddly saw the future with him, but figured it was one my crazy fantasies and that he wouldn't say more than two words to me. Now I know that's not the case. I've found an awesome friend, through all good things and bad. He has great wit and an incredible sense of humor that I've never noticed in that abundance with anybody before. He made me laugh, makes me laugh, and draws me out of my armor by being around me. He has an amazing use of language. All of that I find very attractive. He's well read, curious and inquisitive. I have a serious crush on him. He has a sparkle and bounce to him that I hope he never ever loses, because that's his winning card. He's talented, beautiful, loveable and loving. You want to hold him forever."

Garth grabs Jagger's head whole kissing him hard and then says, "Okay my turn." Garth looks into the camera:

"Well mates, after a seemingly bout of encounters with Jagger I began to feel like a total stalker. However he continues to leave a trail of mystery in his path. His love of earth colored clothes, his compulsion to wear hoodie tops, and that he's interviewed people in bed only to put it in his own work offer more intrigue. Any hesitance to share some of the darker sides of life is totally overridden by the conflict caused by inviting someone into bed where one is most vulnerable. What could possibly make him come up with that concept is another point surrounding my fascination with him.

You don't know what's going on in his mind, but you can see him constantly thinking. It appears complex and too intricate that even he can't verbalize it, because he fears it wouldn't be understood. His voice is like someone peeling paint off a wall. The startling command that it carries as it scratches the surface of sexiness smothering you with the finest seduction. I'm intoxicated with his presence. I had to continue to catch small glimpses of the real and vulnerable "him" kept hidden behind such an immense and impenetrable barrier. I moved cautiously to avoid pressing for revelations of an unpleasant childhood that has perhaps kept him so completely buttoned-up to the outside world. With him is like a dance that is unlike my previous interactions with others that I find myself perhaps rather clumsy in any execution with him. We all have our own protective walls to soften any rejection.

I love the passion that he puts into his writings and in his life in general. It moves me to heights I've never dreamed of with myself. I remember when I was getting to know him I asked, 'What's important to you?' And Jagger glared at me in a staring contest with the most excruciating hesitance before giving fist-punching delivery: "Follow through."

His heart is...well I'm jealous of his heart. He's a charming conundrum, an enigmatic homeless being to which you can attach only vague identity. Whether he is a prince or pauper, gentleman or gypsy remains a mystery. Only know that he bewitches me in an exotic spell. You become helpless to sever yourself from his web where you discover he's had more control over you than you've even realized."

Jagger laughs, "Hey, that's not fair. You said more than I did. We have got to do this again."

Jagger reaches over to the camera to stop it, but not before Garth grabs him. "No, babe. Then we say 'I DO.'"

"Alright I do." Jagger chuckles.

Garth puts his arm around him and they fall into another kiss.

Painting by artist, Joshua Shotwell

"Soul Mates and Twin Flames:

Attracting in Love, Friendships and the Human Heart"

Everyone is interested in love and relationships whether they like to admit it or not. Even the most hardened human soul has fantasized about having a love interest or a partner in crime. One of the main reasons you are here is to love and to learn how to love. This is not just in intimate relationships, but with everyone you come into contact with. In, Soul Mates and Twin Flames: Attracting in Love, Friendships and the Human Heart, author Kevin Hunter touches on the topic of love and relationships by passing on some of the messages and guidance he has received from his own Guides and Angels on the topic. Included in this informational book are some of the basics on, Soul Mates, Twin Flames, Dysfunctional Relationships, Reconnecting with an Ex, Karmic Relationships, Friendships, Loneliness, working with the Romance Angels, Dating, Relationships and more!

"Warrior of Light:
Messages from my Guides and Angels"

There are legions of angels, spirit guides, and departed loved ones in heaven that watch and guide you on your journey here on Earth. They are around to make your life easier and less stressful. Do you pay attention to the nudges, guidance, and messages given to you? There are many who live lives full of negativity and stress while trying to make ends meet. This can shake your faith as it leads you down paths of addictions, unhealthy life choices, and negative relationship connections. Learn how you can recognize the guidance of your own Spirit team of guides and angels around you.

Author, Kevin Hunter, relays heavenly guided messages about getting humanity, the world, and yourself into shape. He delivers the guidance passed onto him by his own Spirit team on how to fine tune your body, soul and raise your vibration. Doing this can help you gain hope and faith in your own life in order to start attracting in more abundance.

Available in paperback and e-book by Kevin Hunter,

"Empowering Spirit Wisdom:
A Warrior of Light's Guide on Love, Career and the Spirit World"

Kevin Hunter relays heavenly, guided messages for everyday life concerns with his book, *Empowering Spirit Wisdom*. Some of the topics covered are your soul, spirit and the power of the light, laws of attraction, finding meaningful work, transforming your professional and personal life, navigating through the various stages of dating and love relationships, as well as other practical affirmations and messages from the Archangels. Kevin Hunter passes on the sensible wisdom given to him by his own Spirit team in this inspirational and powerful book. *Empowering Spirit Wisdom* is part two of the Warrior of Light series of books. Part one is called, *Warrior of Light: Messages from my Guides and Angels*.

"REALM OF THE WISE ONE"

In the Spirit Worlds and the dimensions that exist, reside numerous kingdoms that house a plethora of Spirits that inhabit various forms. One of these tribes is called the Wise Ones, a darker breed in the spirit realm who often chooses to incarnate into a human body one lifetime after another for important purposes.

The *Realm of the Wise One* takes you on a magical journey to the spirit world where the Wise Ones dwell. This is followed with in-depth and detailed information on how to recognize a human soul who has incarnated from the Wise One Realm.

Author, Kevin Hunter, is a Wise One who uses the knowledge passed onto him by his Spirit team of Guides and Angels to relay the wisdom surrounding all things Wise One. He discusses the traits, purposes, gifts, roles, and personalities among other things that make up someone who is a Wise One.

Wise Ones have come in the guises of teachers, shaman, leaders, hunters, mediums, entertainers and others. *Realm of the Wise One* is an informational guide devoted to the tribe of the Wise Ones, both in human form and on the other side.

The biggest cause of turmoil and conflict in one's life is executed by the human ego. All souls have an ego. The most unruly and destructive ego exists within every human soul. When the soul enters into a physical human body, the ego immediately compresses and then swells up. It is the higher self's goal to ensure that it remains in check while living an Earthly life. The ego is what tests each soul along its journey. It is how one learns right from wrong. The experiences and challenges that the soul has while living in this Earthly life school contribute to the soul's growth. When a soul learns lessons, it is intended and expected to grow and enhance from the experience. Yet, there are a great many souls who do not learn lessons and remain in the same spot. The ill of the bunch wreaks all kinds of havoc, destruction, judgment and heart ache in its wake. In *Darkness of Ego*, author Kevin Hunter infuses some of the guidance, messages, and wisdom he's received from his Spirit team surrounding all things ego related. The ego is one of the most damaging culprits in human life. Therefore it is essential to understand the nature of the beast in order to navigate gracefully out of it when it spins out of control. Some of the topics covered in *Darkness of Ego* are humanity's destruction, mass hysteria, karmic debt, and the power of the mind, heaven's gate, the ego's war on love and relationships, and much more.

Also available in paperback and e-book by Kevin Hunter,

"REACHING FOR THE WARRIOR WITHIN"

Reaching for the Warrior Within is the author's personal story recounting a volatile childhood. This led him to a path of addictions, anxiety and overindulgence in alcohol, drugs, cigarettes and destructive relationships. As a survival mechanism he split into different "selves". He credits turning his life around, not by therapy, but by simultaneously paying attention to the messages he has been receiving from his Spirit team in Heaven since birth. He explains how he was able to tell the difference between when his higher self was intervening and ruling the show, and when his lower self was running his life into the gutter.

Reaching for the Warrior Within attests that anyone can change if they pay attention to their own inner guidance system and take action. This can be from being a victim of child abuse, or a drug and alcohol user, to going after the jobs and relationships you want. This powerful story is for those seeking motivation to change, alter and empower their life one day at a time.

"Paint the Silence"

Ruston Bock is a gifted, telepathic sleuth with a drinking problem. Trinity Foyer is a confident detective in New Orleans who has a penchant for dating the wrong men. She requests Ruston's insight into catching a masked serial killer who beheads his victims with an axe made out of car parts. Ruston heads to the city of New Orleans in the middle of a hurricane with his troublesome girlfriend Donna. They come into contact with the eccentric Granger family and the mysteriously cool Logan Granger. Ruston discovers the Granger Mansion holds a wealth of disturbing secrets that can bring the city's real killer to justice.

The *Warrior of Light* series of mini-pocket books are available in paperback and E-book by Kevin Hunter called, *Spirit Guides and Angels, Soul Mates and Twin Flames, Divine Messages for Humanity, Raising Your Vibration, Connecting with the Archangels*

Also available in paperback and E-book by Kevin Hunter, *Ignite Your Inner Life Force, Awaken Your Creative Spirit* and *The Seven Deadly Sins*

ABOUT THE AUTHOR

Kevin Hunter is an author, love expert and channeler. His books tackle a variety of genres and tend to have a strong male protagonist. The messages and themes he weaves in his work surround Spirit's own communications of love and respect which he channels and infuses into his writing and stories.

His books include the *Warrior of Light series of books, Warrior of Light, Empowering Spirit Wisdom, Realm of the Wise One, Reaching for the Warrior Within, Darkness of Ego, Ignite Your Inner Life Force, Awaken Your Creative Spirit,* and *The Seven Deadly Sins.* He is also the author of the horror, drama, *Paint the Silence,* and the modern day erotic love story, *Jagger's Revolution.*

Before writing books and stories, Kevin started out in the entertainment business in 1996 becoming actress Michelle Pfeiffer's personal development dude for her boutique production company, Via Rosa Productions. She dissolved her company after several years and he made a move into coordinating film productions for the big studios on such films as *One Fine Day, A Thousand Acres, The Deep End of the Ocean, Crazy in Alabama, Original Sin, The Perfect Storm, Harry Potter & the Sorcerer's Stone, Dr. Dolittle 2* and *Carolina.* He considers himself a beach bum born and raised in Los Angeles, California.

For more information, www.kevin-hunter.com

~

"Wow! I just read *"Jagger's Revolution"*. Hot! Yum! It's almost like a jerk off reading."

"I hate reading, but this was the first book I actually finished all the way through since High School. It was great."

"This book rocked my soul truly. I loved it."

"It is hot over here and that book of yours only inflames things more."

"This book was making me moist. I had to put it down because I was on a plane. It was embarrassing."

"*Jagger's Revolution* was a beautiful story."

"I finished reading *Jagger's Revolution*. I almost felt guilty reading some of it. I was trying to come at it from an analytical perspective, but I couldn't help but become secretly aroused by Jagger and his friends."

"This book sort of gave me a 'Rebel Without a Cause" feel, but with a lot more penetration. That wasn't a bad feeling."

"I love Jagger tearing around the corner. That guy is so hot. I want one."

"I read your book and I get hard, then I get flaccid, then hard again. You say something that makes you stop and think, then it switches gears and I get hard again."

"Eww you have sex with girls in your book. Yuck! But the Billy sex! Mmm! Instant hard on reading."

"I read your book and it was really good by the way."

"Wow *Jagger's Revolution* was kind of a gay book, but with a sex and the city edge. Loved it!"

"Crawling under the sheets is an expression loosely used to describe that instance where you bare all, but you took it one step further with this book."

"Nice transition at the coffee shop into Slade. I heard the voicemail beep and it was Slade. I had to read to find out who he is!!"

"Love your book!! Awesome erotic stuff :) but you probably get that a lot."

"Was impressed by the books eloquence and passion."

"When you say gay friendships missing morality and loyalty. Kevin you are right I agree."

"Billy and Jagger. Hot scene Kevin. I had visuals"